steven camden

STAND UP FERRAN BURKE

MACMILLAN

Published 2023 by Macmillan Children's Books
an imprint of Pan Macmillan
The Smithson, 6 Briset Street, London EC1M 5NR
EU representative: Macmillan Publishers Ireland Ltd, 1st Floor,
The Liffey Trust Centre, 117–126 Sheriff Street Upper
Dublin 1, D01 YC43
Associated companies throughout the world
www.panmacmillan.com

ISBN 978-1-5290-6776-7

1 3 5 7 9 8 6 4 2

A CIP catalogue record for this book is available from the British Library.

Printed and bound by CPI Group (UK) Ltd, Croydon CR0 4YY

STAND UP
FERRAN BURKE

other books by Steven Camden

everything all at once

my big mouth

summer school and cyborgs

For Jenny,

so proud of you sis

'It was the Dukes'

I have a good memory
moments
things I saw
what people said
tastes and smells
thoughts and feelings
dreams

sometimes
it's like I'm right there
living it again
other times it feels like
I'm watching
somebody else's life

It's crazy how much happens
when you think about it
all the pieces
over all the years   that add up to
who you
are

'Stand up Ferran Burke'.

Year 7 to Year 11

YEAR 7.

where nobody tells you anything so you're
always the last to know.

Playlist.

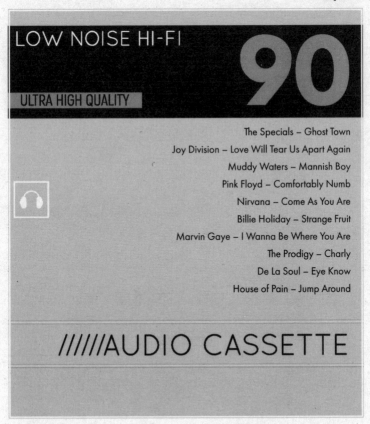

LOW NOISE HI-FI

90

ULTRA HIGH QUALITY

The Specials – Ghost Town
Joy Division – Love Will Tear Us Apart Again
Muddy Waters – Mannish Boy
Pink Floyd – Comfortably Numb
Nirvana – Come As You Are
Billie Holiday – Strange Fruit
Marvin Gaye – I Wanna Be Where You Are
The Prodigy – Charly
De La Soul – Eye Know
House of Pain – Jump Around

//////AUDIO CASSETTE

This Town. (—means somebody not speaking on purpose)

What about in the playground?
No
The lunch hall?
No
But what if I need help?
Ask a teacher
I don't know any teachers
—
Emile?
Okay, if you're completely stuck then you come to me, but only if
I'm by myself. Not if I'm with people
Why not?
Because that's the rules, Ferran
—
Look. You need to carve your own way, without me hanging over
you. Understand?
No
You will. I'll meet you at the gates after last bell, alright?
—

Look at your tie, man

What's wrong with it?

You look like one of The Specials

I like The Specials

That's not how you do it. Come here. Stay still. Did Mom give you lunch money?

Dad did

Cool. Right, you go ahead

What, by myself?

You'll be fine. It's just school.

The Hunt.

Nobody is doing anything
the kid is on the floor, his nose is bleeding and
people are   just watching
walls of them blocking
either side
in case teachers come
I don't know his name, but he was sitting in front
of me in English this morning
now he's on the floor
crying and bleeding and
they've got his lunch money
probably for the rest of his life

He didn't do anything
he was just alone
it was like one of those nature programs where the
hyenas wait for the weakest gazelle to separate   from the pack
then take it down

that could be me

singled out
picked off   and
slaughtered

man

secondary school is different.

me and me and Mom and Dod
Cak

ferran. Year 2

Ms Martin.

'Handsome family'.

Awkward. But at least I know I'm not in trouble.

'I like to try and meet all the new starters who come by themselves.
Especially the ones with older siblings'. Her copper hair looks like
honeycomb next to her pale skin.

Her spider plant takes up half the windowsill.

'It's Kenyan', she says, following my eyes to the orange and black
zig-zaggy wall hanging,

'Amazing country'.

A long black wooden mask stares at me.

'Cool'.

'Year seven can feel very intense at first, especially when you're
flying solo. You're the only one from your primary school who
came here, right'.

'I'm here because Emile is here'.

She nods.

There are two half empty mugs of coffee next to her keyboard.

'I've taught your brother. A very special boy. It's a shame we're losing him for sixth form, although with his gifts, I understand him choosing King Edwards'.

Surprise, surprise. Another full fledged member of the Emile Burke fan club.

She picks at a plaster on her thumb.

'So, what's your thing, Ferran? Are you a Historian like Emile?'

He would love to know she called him a historian. I shrug.

'All in good time', she says, 'For now just concentrate on finding your tribe'.

'My tribe?'

'The people you feel good with. They're here somewhere, I promise. You just need to find them'.

'Okay'.

'Great. And remember my door is always open if you need me'

She seems alright.

Funny how some teachers just seem more like actual people.

Drama.

It's called a trust exercise.
You stand with your arms stretched out, then just fall
back without looking and let your partner
catch you   knowing that if they don't,
you smash your back and head on the floor
Actors do it in rehearsals, she said, it builds bonds
We're not actors
We're brand new year sevens who've only been at the school a
week.
I still don't know anyone except for Emile and I'm not allowed to
speak to him.
Now I'm paired up with a boy I don't know, who has pretty heavy
duty
glasses and a body that a mouse fart could blow over
and I'm supposed to trust him to protect me
from severe spinal injuries and possible brain damage.
'I'll catch you first', I say.
'Okay', he says, like it's no big deal, turning away and spreading
his arms, 'Ready?'

Now I've switched to panicking about not being able to catch him.
He's gonna fall back and I'm gonna drop him and
he's gonna be paralysed and it'll be my fault.
'Hold on, hold on'. Deep breath. 'What's your name by the way?'
'Simon', he says.
'Right. I'm Ferran'.
'I know', he smiles, 'We're in the same form'.
'Don't forget to ask the question', she says, weaving between us,
brushing her long silver hair from her face.
'What's her name again?'
'Miss Lockley', he says, 'You ready?'
'Wait, wait'. I plant my feet and brace myself. 'Okay, I'm ready'.
'Ask the question then'.
'Yeah. Right. Do you trust me, Simon?'
Simon stays facing forward. 'I trust you, Ferran'.
And he falls.

Shoryuken

Ryu floats back down to earth in slow motion
as Sagat arcs through the air and crashes
onto his back
You win. Perfect.
Emile smiles from his bed. It's Friday night. I'm on the floor
watching him play *Street Fighter II*.
Downstairs Mom and Dad are fighting again.
We kept his bedroom door slightly open so we'd know who storms
out this time.
Round 2. Chests bounce. *Fight.*
Sagat throws a tiger knee. Voices from downstairs.
You're giving up, Theo! Like you always do
Ryu blocks, but takes damage.
Giving up on what exactly, Nina? Your expectations?
Haduken.
You're impossible to talk to!
Tiger. Ryu back flips to avoid
You call this talking?
Jab. Jab.
Why won't you listen to me!
Heel kick.
Like you're listening to me?
Jab. Jab.
You're impossible
Haduken.
Maybe if you changed the damn record.
A pause, then a plate smashes

Jesus, Nina! What's wrong with you?

Fireball. Fireball. Sagat is dazed

Ryu moves in.

Mom's stomping feet.

Front door slams.

Shoryuken!

Close up dragon punch. Four hit combo. Sagat groans and collapses.

You win.

Emile nods at me. I stretch out a foot and push his door closed.

Dad's muffled voice, growling to himself

'We should go speak to him'.

Emile cracks his knuckles. 'Nah. Let him cool off'.

He's always so calm about it. Like what happens downstairs doesn't
affect his life.

'They're getting worse', I say.

'Yep'.

I wish I was calm like him.

He offers me the joy pad. 'Wanna do M.Bison?'.

I shake my head.

He knows I've never even got past Vega by myself.

Typical big brother gesture

a pinch of flattery, sprinkled on a cup

of bullshit.

Easy.

It's not Emile's fault he's smart.

It's not like he signed up for some Captain America type program and got injected with genius serum and came out as a super brain. He was just born with it. Something in the genetic code blessed him with a brain that's sharper than the average human.

And it's not like he's Guinness Book of World Records smart either.

He didn't memorise the periodic table when he was breast feeding or speak nine languages at nursery. He's never built a robot out of garden tools or cracked NASA launch codes. He just finds stuff easy.

Ever since I can remember, he's just been able to cruise and look good doing it.

Being really good at football probably helps him too.

That's a curve ball for most people. Like anybody who's really smart

has to be Bambi.

The hard kids have to rate him cos he's captain of the team and the boffins have to rate him cos he can beat five of them at once at chess.

He's a unicorn.

Cooler than most people with no reason to shout about it.

Hard to stay annoyed at somebody like that.

Hard to not feel proud.

And really really really   really hard

to have to follow.

Bluebell.

The smell of pimento
and garlic makes me smile.
Billie Holiday through the speakers at Nan's hushed volume level.
Dexter and Lenny are playing dominoes in their usual
spot by the Double Dragon machine.
Sophia is sipping her red bush tea by the window, deep in her
book.
Nan is opening tins of condensed milk at the counter.
Patrick is watching her from the back corner, over the top of his
paperback and
I feel my body
            relax.
'Brother Ferran! Long time.' Dexter salutes me, tapping his
perfectly angled fedora.
'Yes, Dexter. Still winning?'
He flashes me a smile then slams down a double two and erupts
into laughter. Lenny looks at the table then checks his own hand in
confusion

'Is how you hold that so long?'

He knocks the table top in resignation. Dexter gently lays his last domino and brushes his palms.

'Some of us is just special, ain't it right, brother Ferran?'

'I guess so', I say, dropping my stuff by the stereo and lifting the counter to step through.

'Hey, Nan'.

'Good timing, stranger', she says, handing me a peeler and pointing at a big bag of carrots on the side, 'Juice fi mek'.

I wash my hands in the deep sink. 'Is Dad here?'

She nods to the back door. 'Outside. You want pattie?'

'Chicken please'.

She takes one from the glass cabinet and puts it on a plate next to me.

I go to pick it up and she cuts me a look.

'Carrots first'.

I do what I'm told and get to peeling.

Safety in Numbers.

It's me, Simon and a boy called Pavinder
we've had all lesson to create a scene that shows a family
to share back to the class.
We haven't got anything.
The pair of them have just been talking
about *The Hitchhiker's Guide to the Galaxy*.
Miss Lockley is doing Thai Chi behind her desk.
'We've only got five minutes left', I say, pointing at the clock.
Pav nods, his black hair is LEGO figure neat.
Simon takes off his shoes and kneels on them like his legs are tiny.
'I'm the baby. We're in the supermarket'.
He wails. The girls nearest to us look over.
'One of you has to be the Dad'.
Pav looks at me.
I think of Dad and feel myself frowning.
'Perfect!', says Si, 'Dad's hate shopping. Pav, you're the mom'.
Pav looks at me again.
I shrug.
'Oh no, quick!', says Simon, pouting, 'Baby needs poo poo!'
and all three of us
laugh.

As a friend, as a friend
As an old enemy
— K. Cobain

18

Fork.

It's lunch time in the cafeteria.

Different years sit with their own.

The three of us are sitting at the year seven table eating chips and peas.

Si and Pav are having the Megadrive vs Super Nintendo argument again.

On the furthest table by the fire escape, I can see Emile with some other year elevens, laughing and joking. The teacher's table is next to theirs. Mr Cage the head of lower school and History is talking with the others, but he's watching Emile.

'Sonic alone means Megadrive wins'

'You're drunk, Si. It's not even close. *Mario Kart*. Zelda. Shall I go on? Tell him, Ferran'

I eat my chips, watching Cage hawking Emile. 'He's right, Si. Nintendo all day'.

Out of nowhere a fork goes flying up from Emile's table.

It spins through the air over heads, hits the floor and slides under the piano.

Cage is up in a flash. 'Emile Burke!'

The whole cafeteria goes quiet.

Emile looks at his friends. It wasn't him who did it.

'Burke! Stand up, right now!'

Emile stands.

Simon nudges me. 'Isn't that your brother?'

I don't answer.

Cage strides over to Emile and gets in his face.

'Can you explain to me why you want to endanger the rest of us with flying forks?'

Emile doesn't speak.

'Do you think it's funny?'

'It wasn't him', I say under my breath, 'Tell him it wasn't you'.

Emile just stands there. Cage leans right over him. 'Well?'

Another year eleven boy stands up, 'It wasn't him, sir. It was me'.

'Sit down, Williams, I saw who did it', his eyes don't leave Emile.

The other boy looks at Emile and sits down. I want to stand up and scream.

Emile sighs, 'It was an accident. Sorry, sir'.

I don't get why he's just taking it.

'Well, I think we all deserve an apology', sneers Cage 'Seen as how you could have blinded one of us'.

He grabs Emile's shoulders and flips him round to face the room.

Emile scans everyone. I hide behind Pav.

'I'm sorry everyone', says Emile.

Cage leans over him, 'Louder'.

'I'm sorry everyone!'

Cage points towards the piano. 'Now, go and fetch it'.

There's a second, and I get myself ready.

This is where Emile spins round and tell him to fetch it himself, to fetch it and shove it right up his arse. He was just building the tension.

Emile doesn't say anything,
he just walks over and squats down, fishing the fork
out while the whole cafeteria watches
and brings it back to the table.
It's like he's pretending to be somebody else. Somebody normal.
Cage snatches the fork from him. 'We'll discuss cafeteria safety in
detention. My room at the end of the day. Everyone, back to your
lunches!'
He goes back to the teacher's table. Emile sits down with his
friends. The cafeteria rumbles back into life.
'That guy is psycho', says Pav.
'Yeah', says Simon, 'I heard he locks you in his cupboard if you talk
back. You gonna eat those chips, Ferran?'
My skin feels hot. I slide my plate towards him.
'Nah. I'm done'.

History.

Nan and Pops opened The Bluebell in the early 70s when Dad and
aunty Marsha were kids.
For a while it was a real centre for the Caribbean community
in the area. They'd have meetings upstairs and Nan let local
photographers and artists put their pictures on the wall to sell.
We all used to come every Sunday afternoon to eat brown stewed
chicken and hang out while Pops and the other old guys in their
crisp suits sat jamming on the raised corner stage til past bedtime.
Mom took photos that Nan put up, but Dad took them down after
Pops died last year.
Now it's just one of Pop's on his drums and the same faded decor
since back in the day, including the small handful of regulars
clinging on.
Dad tidied up the back yard and sometimes gives talks with young
musicians
when he's not at the college, helping them with their demos
and boring them stupid with lectures about the poisonous music
industry.

Bouncer.

We're eating fish finger sandwiches watching *Neighbours*.
Lucy Robinson has just realised her sight has come back after the accident.
It's dark outside, but the curtains are open. Mom and Dad aren't home yet.
'What's his problem?' I say.
'Who?'
'Cage'.
Emile wipes up ketchup with his crust, 'He's just a teacher'.
'He's just a dick head'.
Emile chuckles through a full mouth. 'Maybe you should tell him'.
'Why didn't you? With the fork?'
He looks at me. 'You saw that?'
I nod. Emile looks back at the screen. Jim Robinson thinks that Lucy is still blind.
Only Bouncer the dog knows she isn't.
'Are other teachers like that with you?'
'Not all of them'
'Is it because you're smart?'
'It's because I'm not meant to be'.
I don't understand. Emile can tell. 'Smart is just being yourself, and nobody else'.
It sounds like something Nan would say.
Lucy Robinson is looking at herself in the mirror, deciding what to do.
'Somebody should tell him he's a full prick'.
Emile laughs as he pulls the curtains closed, 'Maybe it's you, little

brother. Maybe you're the one'. He takes my empty plate. His top lip is starting to darken from hairs.

'Choc ice?'

'Yes, please'.

He goes to the kitchen.

Lucy Robinson is pretending she's still blind so people treat her like she is and

I know it's wrong

but I get it.

DAILY NEWS

World - Business - Finance - Lifestyle - Travel - Sport - Weather

Issue: 240104   THE WORLDS BEST SELLING NATIONAL NEWSPAPER   Est - 1965

First Edition   Monday 5th June

Local Boy Breaks Scoring Record.

Fifteen year old Emile Burke of Wakens Tip High School in Sandwell has smashed the previous secondary school football league record for goals scored, notching up 114 goals in a single season that saw Wakens Tip take home the district trophy.

When asked how he felt, the calm and collected youngster simply said, 'I play up front. That's my job'.

Sheep's Eye.

It's morning break.

I'm on the bench watching the Royal Rumble
of other year sevens playing football while Si and Pav argue next
to me.

Next lesson we're supposed to dissect a sheep's eye.

'You're gonna have eye juice on your face'.

'Shut up. It shouldn't be legal. I'm not doing it. They can't make
me'.

'I thought you wanted to be a doctor'.

'Not that kind of doctor. Ferran tell him to stop'.

'Leave it, Si. You're scared too'.

'No I'm not! I love cutting stuff up. I helped my Dad gut some fish
once'.

I miss football. All we ever do at break time is sit and talk about
nothing.

'We should go and play', I say.

The pair of them look at each other, then laugh.

'Yeah, right. Good one, Ferran'.

A boy called Taylor and his sidekick Jordan are running the game. I
know them from P.E.

A smaller boy with dark hair and eyebrows is in goal.

Taylor takes a shot, the boy makes an awesome save, tipping it up
onto the fence higher than the cross bar. Taylor celebrates like he
scored anyway. The boy says something.

Next thing, Taylor and Jordan are right in his face.

'He saved it', I say.

Taylor pushes the boy into the fence and he falls down.

A crowd forms around them and starts to shout.

'Leave him alone'.

'Leave who alone?' says Si.

'The boy. In goal. Taylor's gonna stomp him', I stand up, 'He didn't do anything'.

'Taylor? So what? It's nothing to do with us'.

'He didn't do anything'. I start to walk towards the cage.

'Ferran! Don't be dumb. You wanna get beat up too?'

Pav is shaking his head.

The bell goes and the crowd starts to break up.

Taylor and Jordan are laughing to each other as they walk off.

Si and Pav head towards science.

As I pass the cage, I watch the boy pick himself up and dust himself down.

The side of his face is grazed.

As he puts on his bag he looks at me through the mesh. I nod.

He mouths two words.

Piss off.

Form Room.

Before Miss arrives
it's always pure chaos with
everyone shouting and laughing and
playing table football with
pennies and
stealing pencil cases and calling
each other dickhead and
giving slaps and
in the middle of it all there's
this one girl with
short black
hair and a round face called Michelle who
always sits
by herself
reading comics
like she's in a silent
bubble of total calm that
nobody else
can burst

Cola cubes.

Emile is talking to a really pretty sixth former.

She has big eyes and holds her folders next to her chest.

I'm nervous as I approach them. It's not the school gates and I know the rules.

Emile sees me. 'Here he is!'

His top half is uniform, bottom half football kit. 'What kept you?'

He's playing the caring older brother.

'I'm Milly', she says. I freeze. She's even prettier close up. Her cheeks are round and she has tiny diamond studs in her ears. Emile slaps my shoulder.

'This is Ferran. He's brand new'.

Milly tilts her head. 'He's a cutey'.

I nearly wet myself.

'Cuter than me?' says Emile. They share a smile and start towards the gates.

I check my trousers and walk after them.

We cross the road to walk in the sun.

They're talking about Emile leaving school at the end of the year to go to the fancy sixth form. Milly is teasing him about thinking he's better than everyone else.

Emile is pretending he doesn't. He tells her she looks like Donna from *Twin Peaks*. She doesn't know who that is. There might be a party happening. I can't hear where or when.

Milly has cola cubes.

She offers me one and I accidentally take two.

She doesn't notice.

She keeps asking to touch Emile's hair.

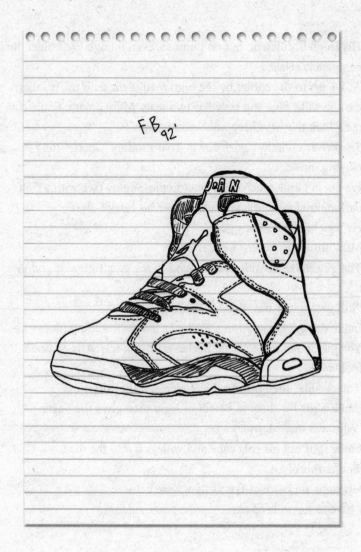

His laugh is different, but on purpose. Even though she's older, he's completely relaxed.

As we get to the corner by the high road, a car pulls up. It's that dark metallic blue and only has two seats. Milly groans. Emile cuts me a look that says keep your mouth shut.

The driver's window goes down. That Prodigy 'Charly' song is playing inside.

He doesn't look much older than Emile. Skinny face with a thin dark moustache and a gold chain over his black t-shirt.

He taps his wrist. 'Let's go, Mill'.

Milly shrugs to Emile, 'I better go'.

The guy stares as Milly walks round to the passenger side and gets in.

'Still getting the bus, Burke?' He laughs.

Emile doesn't say anything. He looks like he's holding his breath.

The guy looks at me. 'Little Burke, is it?' I'm scared, but I don't look away.

'Laters, kids', then he revs the engine and they drive off.

Emile waits for them to be out of sight then gives the finger.

'Who was that?' I say.

Emile spits out his cola cube and volleys it into the road.

'Forget this place'.

His steps are twice as fast as they were before.

I have to jog to keep up.

A Friend. (– means someone not speaking on purpose)

Did your Dad speak to you?
About what?
About me and him
No
Of course not
–

We've been talking
We heard. The whole street did
Oh
You're leaving, right?
No! I'm not leaving
You're moving out
Yes. I am. It's for the best, for everyone
–

Is that a new poster?
No
Oh
–

It's been coming for a while, love
Yeah
–

Where will you go?
To a friend's place, for a little bit. I won't be far
A friend?
–

–

What do you think?

About what?

Ferran

I don't know. What am I supposed to think? What did Emile say?

Your brother said he understands

Right

It's for the best

You said that

–

–

Is there anything you want to ask?

Like what?

Like anything

–

We love you both very much, me and your dad. Things just need to change.

Why?

People need to try and be happy, Ferran. Life is short

Are you not happy?

–

Are you having an affair?

My love

But you're in love with someone else, right?

–

Who is he?

Ferran, it's not that simple. I wish it were that simple. Relationships are complicated. People change. What people want changes.

Do you love Dad?

Of course I do. Your Dad and me will always love each other. In a way.

In a way that means you don't really like each other
You're a smart boy
—

My two smart boys

Viens avec moi –	Come with me
Tu me manques –	I miss you
Tu as raison –	You are right
Bonne idée –	Good idea
Je comprends –	I understand
Je suis pret –	I am ready
Je ne sais pas –	I don't know
Ce n'est pas vrai –	This is not true

8/8
Tres bien, Ferran!

Stocks.

A boy called Tyler in my year five class had parents who
were divorced.
He always used to brag about having two birthdays and
two Christmases.
The rest of us used to say that we hoped our parents
split up too. That it would be worth it for the extra presents.
We weren't really thinking
about what we were saying.
You say a lot of stupid stuff in juniors.

And Rising.

'I know you're pissed off with me'

We're driving back from the chippy. I've got the hot paper bag in my lap.

Dad's put the De La Soul album on. He thinks it's my favourite.

'Come on, say your piece', he says, like I'm some old buddy he grew up with.

I stare out of my window. The smell of salt and vinegar.

We've had take away every night for a week. Mom would be furious.

'Fine', he says, 'Your brother won't speak to me either'.

We turn onto our road.

'It takes two to tango, Ferran. Just remember that'.

'Nobody's dancing, Dad'.

We both double take. Emile usually has all the good lines. Dad pulls up and turns the engine off. The music cuts out. He keeps his eyes forward.

'What are you gonna do?' I say.

He just shrugs. 'She's made her choice'.

I wanna grab him and shake him. Kick him back to life.

'Did she tell you about him?' he says.

'Tell me what?'

He won't look at me. I swallow a scream.

'Nobody tells me shit!'

For a brief moment, time seems to skip. I've sworn before, but never directly at him.

I prep myself for him to shout. I almost want it.

Dad just frowns, then gets out of the car.

It's like this whole situation has somehow
changed the rules.

BFF.

'Best friends forever'.
We're in Si's bedroom.
It's twice the size of mine with a hamburger beanbag and
massive framed periodic table on the wall.
Me and Pav have already rolled out our sleeping bags and
there's still empty floor space by the window.
His comic collection is two shelves deep and
he has his own double bed which is nuts.
Pav takes Si's hand and crosses his free one over it 'Best friends
forever'.
I cross my hands and take both of theirs, completing the triangle.
'Best friends forever', and we do the secret shake.
It's two weeks before Christmas.
We've been playing *Streets of Rage* on Si's megadrive and now it's
Nintendo time.
Later we'll watch Batman and eat popcorn and
stay up talking about what the coolest job in the world would be
and
they'll both agree it would be making computer games and I'll say
I'm not sure and they'll both fall asleep first.
I'll lie on my back, listening to Pav gently snoring, and I'll
remember

Ms Martin talking about finding your tribe and I'll wonder
if I have and then, as the light from passing cars
slides across the periodic table, I'll wonder
where Mom is and who
she's with.

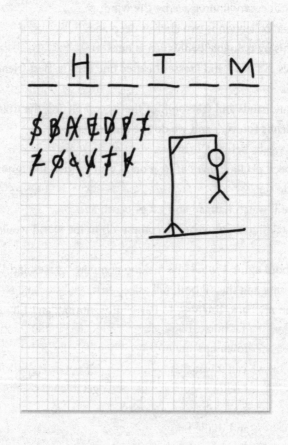

Contestant Number Two.

Crisps and ham sandwiches with too much butter
watching *Blind Date* in Wakefield.
I'm drinking dandelion and burdock. Emile says it tastes like
toothpaste so he's just got water.
Granddad Phillip and Nana Barbara's house is a bungalow
in a quiet cul de sac of other bungalows.
When we were little, Emile used to call it Castle Boring.
Everything is either pale pink or beige and it smells like shake 'n'
vac.
The only thing that used to save it
was Daniel, their Jack Russell, but it turns out when Jack Russells
get old,
they hate people.
We didn't want to come, but Mom and Dad wouldn't be in the
same house so we're here til Boxing Day when Mom drops us
back.
It feels weird knowing we won't be with Dad on Christmas day,
but he'll be with Nan so at least he's not alone.
Daniel is sitting in front of the fire like a pissed off sphinx.
Everything looks the same. Little plastic tree with one skinny
silver snake of tinsel. The long grandfather clock. Nana Barbara's
painting of the fat horse. Baby photos of me and Emile.
          The 'grown ups' are in the kitchen, talking about Dad.
They think we can't hear them.
Nana Barbara is telling Mom she needs to get a lawyer. Granddad
Phillip is asking
how much me and Emile know.

On the TV, a man in a cream suit is demonstrating his tango skills
for Cilla and the crowd.

Emile turns it up.

'Turn it down', I whisper, 'I want to hear them'.

'I don't'. He throws a chunk of his sandwich to Daniel, who
gobbles it up.

'How much do you know?' I say.

'What's to know? They can't be together, so they're gonna be
apart. Simple', He throws Daniel another chunk, 'At least she's
undermining stereotypes. Everybody always assumes it's the black
guy who screws around'.

He smiles like it's a joke. My stomach knots. 'Don't you care?'

'Would you rather live in a house with them constantly fighting?'

'Yes!'

'Oh, grow up, Ferran'.

I hate it when he says that. Daniel wants my food. On the TV, Our
Graham is giving us a quick reminder.

'Why aren't you even sad?'

Daniel shuffles over to my feet and whines. Emile ignores me and
drinks the last of his crisps.

The man in the cream suit waves goodbye to the crowd,
the woman went with contestant number two.

I slide the rest of my sandwich onto the floor and watch Daniel
go to work.

6 Hours later...

We're top to toe in the spare room double bed.

Emile tried to make me sleep on the floor, but I told

Mom and she made him share the mattress.

It feels like it's been eleven o clock for six hours.

Granddad Phillip made us all sit through *High Noon* again, then fell
asleep half way through.

We ate mince pies and played Monopoly. Emile got Park Lane and
Mayfair and nobody said a single word about Dad.

I'm listening to The Best of Talking Heads on my Walkman.

I took it from Dad's car. In one of the songs the singer says 'I can't
seem to face up to the facts' and it's like he's talking to me.

Emile is reading one of Nana's Mills & Boon novels, searching for
the sexy bits.

When he finds one, he kicks me to take off my headphones and
whispers about Heathcliff's swollen member and Emily's heaving
bosom just to make me squirm.

Later, when he thinks I'm asleep,

I feel the bed rocking and hear him breathing heavily.

When making a B.L.T always use the lettuce as a buffer to stop the tomato making the bread soggy.

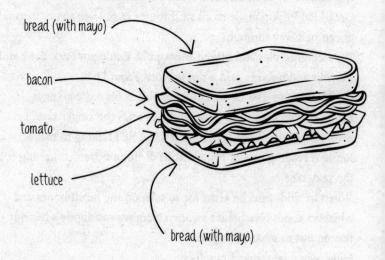

bread (with mayo)

bacon

tomato

lettuce

bread (with mayo)

Footlocker.

'I don't think so' says Mom.
We're standing in front of the trainers and I'm pointing
at the new black Air Jordan 6s with the infrared.
'Jump Around' by House of Pain is booming out from the ceiling
speakers.
They're ninety quid.
With my combined Christmas money I've got fifty.
'How about these?'
She picks up some white Reebok classics. Emile calls them
hooligan shoes. I shake my head.
Mom checks her watch. A stocky girl in the black and white stripes
comes over.
'Do you need help?'
Mom puts the Reeboks back. 'He's looking for trainers'.
I glare at her, 'We're good thanks'.
Mom checks her watch again.
'I need to run a quick errand'.
'Okay, where to?'
'By myself'. She's fidgeting, 'Meet me at the big Waterstones in an
hour?'
'Where are you going?'
'Just to run an errand', she fixes her hair, 'You'll be fine. Choose
something good and don't speak to anyone'.
She kisses me on top of the head and leaves.
I feel my folded envelope of notes in my pocket.
Decisions decisions.

55 minutes later...

Outside Waterstones feeling stupid.
The sky is dark with clouds and my envelope is still full in my pocket.
I couldn't decide on anything. Money has so much potential before you spend it.
I feel the spit of rain and there's no sign of Mom so I go in.
High ceilings and rows and rows of books.
In one corner there's a thin graphic novel section. I go over and quiet Michelle from form is sitting in the corner on a little metal stool.
She's wearing a black duffle coat, hunched over a comic.
We've never really spoken and seeing her in the real world feels weird.
She must be here with someone, nobody
comes into town by them-self.
　　　Emile would go over and ask her what she's reading and then get
　　　into some cool conversation about comics and art. She looks fully engrossed in her book　　　though so I leave it.
I take *Watchmen* off the shelf.

When I asked to read Emile's copy, he said it's too dark for me yet.

The weight of it is really satisfying.

'Classic'.

A pudgy man with a ponytail and patchy beard is standing next to me.

He's wearing one of those dark green army coats with the German flag on the shoulder.

He smells like garden shed.

'Alan Moore is God', he says, scouring the shelves.

I look over and quiet Michelle is staring

right at me, a look of panic on her face.

I'm about to wave when she springs to her feet and darts round the corner out of sight.

I put *Watchmen* back and go after her, but the bookshop crowd is thick and she's gone.

'There you are!'

Mom is holding a takeaway coffee and one of those small fancy cardboard shopping bags with ribbon tying it shut. Her cheeks are flushed.

'Where's your trainers?'

'I don't need any', I say, pointing at her gift, 'Who's that for?'

Mom grips it, smiling like a little girl.

'Me'.

Small Comforts.

The crumbly pastry
the sweet spicy heat of the chicken filling
I close my eyes and
I'm six again
sitting at Nan's kitchen table
eating my pattie as she washes rice

before everything changed
before our family broke apart

I open my eyes and realise
I'm crying.
Nan puts her arm around me and kisses my head
the pattie is warm in my hands
the empty cafe is calm.
'Eat up, soldier', she says, 'Food mek it alright'.

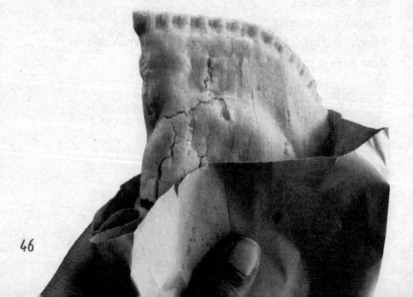

Tuna.

It's bigger than a kitten, but smaller than a proper cat
just sitting there
outside the back door, head tilted, looking up at me.
Black fur with a white chin. No collar.
'What's your name?'
The rain drops quicken. The cat sneezes.
Dad's blasting Pink Floyd upstairs. Feels like he's been up there for days.
I open the back door wider. 'You want to come in?'
It doesn't move.
I leave the door open and fetch a can of tuna out of the cupboard
and drop it onto the last clean
plate. 'Hungry?'
The cat just stares.
I lay the plate on the floor by the open door and go back to the
table,
pretending to do homework.
Upstairs, Pink Floyd turns into Muddy Waters.
When I look back, the plate by the back door is empty.
I go over and pick it up. No cat anywhere.
I close the door and Tetris slot the plate
into the sink full of dirties and there it is,
curled up on my school bag, next to my chair, fast asleep like it's
lived here
all its life.

Cyat. (– means somebody not speaking on purpose).

She must belong to somebody
I don't think so
Is that right?
She doesn't have a collar. I think she's a stray
So you're David Attenborough now?
Nobody's come looking and there's no pictures on lampposts
Sorry, you're Columbo
Dad
Cat Columbo
She needs a home
Yeah, and food and care and probably flea powder
I'll look after her, you won't have to do anything
It's a living thing, Ferran, not a toy
I understand that
Do you? What about Swimmy? Remember Swimmy?
Swimmy was Emile's
He was everyone's. Rest in peace.
Dad I can do this. Please let me keep her. She chose us. It isn't a
coincidence
Your mom doesn't like cats
I know
They make her sneeze
Mom's not here, Dad
–

Animals are good for you
–

They bring good energy

If she pees inside she's gone

Yep

And if she touches my records

She won't. I promise. Thank you. Thank you.

We'll see. What's her name?

—

She needs a name, Ferran. Unless we're just gonna call her Cyat

Tuna. Her name's Tuna

Tuna?

Yep

Okay. Well, good luck, Tuna. I hope you make it.

Head of Year Comments

Ferran has settled in well and proven himself to be a capable and conscientious student. He demonstrates high levels of ability in most subjects and his disciplinary record and attendance are most commendable. He should be proud of his adjustment to secondary school life and I hope his progress continues in the coming years.

Ms JA Martin

House Red.

It's a big round table that you have to spin.
Mom ordered too much. Dad said she was silly.
I'm still surprised he came.
It's the first time all four of us have sat together for months and it's
weird.
I'm building my fifth duck pancake, laying my foundation of
spring onion and cucumber strips. There's a Chinese family at the
big table in the corner. A girl half my age is using chopsticks like
it's nothing. Cliché zheng music is playing really low.
'Pretty fancy, Nina' says Dad, dipping an egg roll in sweet chilli,
'Come here a lot?'
Mom doesn't bite.
'Twelve years old', she says to me, 'Where's my little Ferran gone?'
Emile makes googoo gaga noises. I kick him under the table.
'We should get wine', says Dad, waving the waiter over.
'Not for me, thank you', says Mom, picking at her tiny mound of
rice.
'Watching your weight, Nina?'
Mom frowns.
'No. I mean you look good. I mean'. The waiter arrives and saves
him. Dad orders the house red.
'Are you growing your hair, Ferran?' says Mom.
I shrug. There's hoisin sauce on my fingers.
'He's trying to beat his brother's high top', says Dad.
'No I'm not'.
'Anything to look taller eh, Ferran?' Emile smiles.
I pretend to scratch my chin and give him the finger.

Dad pulls a box from under the table. It's wrapped in a plastic bag.
He puts it next to the noodles and spins the table to me.
'Happy Birthday, son'.
It looks like it might be a thick book. Emile probably told him I
really wanted to read *Lord of The Rings* just to be funny. I haven't
finished a book since *The Outsiders* last term.
'Open it', says Dad as the waiter brings the wine. I look at Emile.
He seems curious.

It's a new Walkman,
and not a cheap one, one of the expensive metal Panasonic ones
with auto reverse and the little plugs that go in your ears.
'No way!' says Emile and his jealousy makes it even sweeter.
'Wow', says Mom, 'Pretty cool'.
Dad can't hide his excitement, 'It's even got a record function with
a little mic. For ideas and you know, when you have them'.
'Thanks, Dad'
'All good. Maybe don't take it out here, don't want to grease it up'.
'Yeah. Right'.
I wrap the plastic bag back round it and put it on the table. I
can see Emile staring at it as he hands me an envelope. 'Happy
Birthday, midget', he says.
The card has Garfield the cat eating lasagne on it. I open it up and
a ten pound note slips out.
'Yo! Thanks, Emile!'
'No big deal', he says.
I read his message and smirk.
'What's it say?' says Mom.
'Use it to buy yourself a personality'.

Dad laughs, Mom tries not to, but cracks when I smile.

'My turn', she says, lifting up a bigger box.

It's too big to put on the table so she hands it to Dad who passes it to me.

The wrapping paper is Snoopy and Woodstock.

'Thanks, Mom'.

'I hope I got the right ones'.

I feel like I'm on stage as the three of them watch me unwrap. My stomach flips when I see the silver jump-man against the black box.

'No way!'

It's the black Air Jordan 6s with the infrared. I actually squeal.

'You've gotta be kidding me!' says Emile as I open the box and lift the tissue paper.

They're beautiful.

The red next to the black suede. The frosted air bubble. The squares in the tongue.

That new trainer smell.

'Happy Birthday, love'.

And a wave of sad crashes over me.

All of this. The four of us. How much has changed.

I breathe deep to stop myself crying. 'Thank you, Mom'.

'Do you know how much they cost?' Emile's jealousy has jumped off the charts, 'They're like-'

Mom glares at him and he shuts up.

'Lucky boy', says Dad, 'Let's toast'.

He pours wine for himself and a small one for Emile, Mom puts
her hand over her glass.

'Suit yourself', he takes mine, 'And a little for the birthday boy'.
He pours less than one finger and hands it to me. I look at Mom.
She smiles and shrugs.

'To Ferran', says Dad. We all lift our glasses and clink. The little
girl with the chopsticks watches. The wine is bitter and coats my
teeth.

'Try them on', says Mom.

'Here?'

'Use the loos. If they're not the right size, we can take them back'.

The toilets are really bright, with shiny white tiles and
a full wall mirror. I sit in the cubicle and slip them on.
They're amazing.
I feel taller.
I fold the bottom of my jeans behind the tongue, tighten
the little toggles on the laces then walk up and down in the mirror
like a catwalk model.
They're the best trainers I've ever had.
I put my old ones in the box under the tissue paper, one last look
in the mirror, then I go back
into the restaurant.

Dad's not there.

Emile is staring at his food.

Mom is wiping her eyes.

'Hey, sweetie, how are they?'

'Where's Dad?'

'He just. He wanted some air'.

'He left', says Emile.

'Why?'

Emile looks at Mom. I put the shoebox on my chair. 'What happened?'

Mom lets out a deep breath.

She looks at Emile, then back at me.

'I've got some news'.

YEAR 8.

where you start to clock how full of it
most people are.

Playlist.

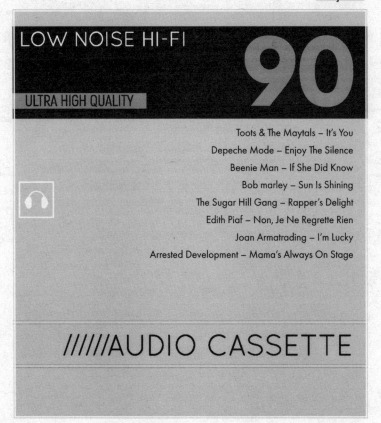

LOW NOISE HI-FI

90

ULTRA HIGH QUALITY

Toots & The Maytals – It's You
Depeche Mode – Enjoy The Silence
Beenie Man – If She Did Know
Bob marley – Sun Is Shining
The Sugar Hill Gang – Rapper's Delight
Edith Piaf – Non, Je Ne Regrette Rien
Joan Armatrading – I'm Lucky
Arrested Development – Mama's Always On Stage

//////AUDIO CASSETTE

Assembly.

Me and Si are front row
Pav is behind with his form group.
The whole of lower school watching Ms Martin give a presentation
about Duke of Edinburgh awards, clicking through slides of
pictures from previous years on the big projector screen.
It's a thing where you go orienteering and canoeing and get badges
or something.
Taylor and them are groaning. Si and Pav are well into it.
Ms Martin clicks and a big picture of Emile abseiling comes up. She
looks at me and smiles.
Even though he's left, he's still here.
'She likes you', Si whispers, when she looks away.
'Shut up'.
When the presentation is done, Mr Cage gets up and goes into a
dry speech about behavioural expectations for the new year. Si
gives me a pained look. We've got him for history.
At one point someone in year nine farts and everyone erupts into
laughter.

Cage sends a whole line outside to wait for him.

The school librarian makes an announcement about
unreturned books and then two girls step out to the front.

One of them is Kayla, from English, but the other girl I've never
seen before.

They giggle nervously as they hold up a photograph of a golden
retriever. They're planning on skipping non stop for six hours to
raise money for the local dog's home. They'll have a bucket and a
list and will be outside reception at break time.

My stomach is dancing. I can't take my eyes off her.

Cage dismisses us and we start to shuffle out row by row.

I check my pockets and nudge Si.

'Yo, how much money you got?'

All I Know. (I hate describing people)

She's new and
has dark hair and
perfect lips and
eyes
like a cat
in a good way and
she does her tie
in a fat chunky knot and
she's always with Kayla at break time drinking tea and
they always say
Oh My Days! And she has
this loud laugh like a cackle
but it's not annoying, it's like
  from the belly and true and
          her skirt fits her perfect and
she sits at the next table in English
she wears black Kickers and
pulls faces at her friends when they
walk past outside and
I haven't spoken to her properly yet but
her name is
Lana Jacobs.

Tea & Biscuits.

I'm in the queue with Pav. Si is saving us a seat over on the tables.
I can smell the warm biscuits through the hatch. Break time bakery
is a new thing.
'Why are we here again?' says Pav.
I look over at Lana with her friends near the front, getting their
teas. 'Tea and biscuits, man'.
'I thought you hated tea?'
'No. I love tea. Shut up'.
I make sure I sit so I can see them as we eat.
Our shortbread biscuits are uneven and heavy, but buttery and
sweet.
The girls are proper loud, laughing and clapping a lot. Pav and Si
quietly sip and nibble.
'You haven't touched your tea', Pav points at my full cup.
'I was letting it cool down', I say, picking it up.
Taylor and Jordan and a few others bowl in from outside, smacking
each other and making fart noises. That kid Cello with the dark
eyes is with them, tagging along at the back.

Si and Pav hunch down.

I take a sip. It's disgusting.

Si dunks his biscuit, 'Did you learn the vocab?' Pav nods.

'Shit', I say, 'I forgot. Can I copy you?'

They both roll their eyes just as Taylor and them walk past.

Someone trips Jordan and he falls into Si, spilling his tea everywhere.

'Dickhead!' shouts Jordan at one of the other goons. Our table is a brown lake.

'Man!' says Pav, 'I'm soaked'.

He immediately regrets it as Jordan steps to him. 'You got a problem?'

Pav shakes his head. Si starts to mop up the tea with napkins.

Jordan digs him in the back, 'Yeah, clean it up, pussy'. The other goons laugh.

I can see Lana and the girls looking over. I want to do some thing.

'What's up, Burke?' Jordan's eyeing me. 'You want some?'

He's shaved a line into one of his eyebrows.

I hold his stare for a second, then help Si
clean up.

Standard.

Every morning on my way
to form I have to walk past Emile's smiling face.
Eleven As.
Maths and English 98% on both papers, History 95%.
They were the best results in the school by miles and only one other girl
in the whole borough did anywhere near as good.
The local paper interviewed them both and the school put the photo up in the reception cabinet
next to the football trophies he won with the team.
Mom was crying. Dad just nodded a lot.
Emile acted like it was nothing special.
Him and his friends covered each other in flour and eggs and bombed the school
with wet toilet roll, but the very next day, he started talking about
A levels and university.
Dad told him to take a second to enjoy what he's achieved. Emile wasn't listening.
He wants three As for his A Levels and to go to uni in London and nobody
is going to bet against him.
He left the little GCSE result slips on the kitchen table
like they were old take away menus.
I got a look as I ate my shredded wheat.
The long line of As on the paper looked like the sound of somebody screaming.

Double Geography.

We're supposed to be plotting
a map between school and our houses
Si and Pav are sharing one ruler
getting well into it because they both live the same way.
Our house is in the opposite direction and I feel
like the third wheel they don't really need
or maybe I'm the unicycle and
they're the stabilisers
I'm not sure
these are the kind of thoughts I keep
to myself
thoughts like, unless I join the army (not happening)
when in my real life am I ever gonna need
to draw a map to scale? Or
identify a site of long shore drift?
Thoughts like
who cares
if that cloud is cumulonimbus? Or what kind of rock
you find on the beaches in Devon?
What I would like to know is
if everyone in here yawned
at exactly the same time could
we suck enough oxygen out
of the room to make sir
pass out
so I could just press play on my Walkman, sit back
and wait for the bell?

The More I Give.

Toots & The Maytals means
Patrick has control of the stereo.
He's the only one Nan will allow to use it and
he only gets to choose when he's cooking.
He's Irish, but he cooks yard food good as anyone.
I'm watching him undress spring onions and smoosh
garlic with salt ready for Saturday soup.

He moves smoothly around the kitchen, humming along to
'Funky Kingston'.
Usually I'd be helping, but I have homework that's overdue.
I rarely come on weekends these days, but I can't work at home
with Dad moping around.

Dexter and Lenny are at the dominoes table sipping
dragon stout as they play.

Sophia is reading sheet music by the window.
'How's school then?' says Patrick, reaching for a jar of pimento
seeds.
There's a blurry blue word tattooed on his inside forearm.
I hold up my copy of *Romeo & Juliet*, 'Great, yeah'
Patrick nods, 'Ah, Tragedy', he crunches the seeds with his knife
handle, 'That's a good one'.

Lenny gives a loud groan. Dexter's won another game.

'Do you want to read it for me?' I say, 'I can't make any sense of it'.

Patrick smiles and lifts his knife like a torch.

'My bounty is as boundless as the sea, my love as deep, the more I give to thee, the more I have',

he pauses, 'Nope. I don't remember the rest. Long time ago now'.

He goes back to cooking. I have so many questions.

Nan comes back in carrying her window cleaning bucket.

'They look spotless', says Patrick.

Nan wipes her forehead. 'It soon dutty again'.

She watches him dice the lamb.

'Remember fi skim the scum this time. Nobody want soup taste like foot'

'Yes, Ella'. He flashes me a smile as he moves out of her way.

Nan pours her bucket water into the sink and arches her back.

'This country mek mi creak'.

'Can I do anything to help, Nan?'

'You just fix on the books so you no affi clean windows all day', she scowls at Patrick,

'You never even offer the boy a drink?'

She kisses her teeth and goes to the fridge.

Patrick smiles again and keeps chopping.

Nan puts a cola Champagne on my table and stares at me. 'Look at me'

'What is it?'

She lifts my chin like a doctor and narrows her eyes. 'You in love?'

'What? No!'

She looks at Patrick. Patrick shrugs.

'I'm not!'

Nan smiles. 'No. Course not'.

BOYS	GIRLS
LUCAS	MONA
CASEY	YASMIN
~~BOBBY~~	SADIE

What Light Through Yonder.

Equal parts terrified and praying.

He's putting boys with girls to read sections from the play.

A girl called Jodie told him that he was being gender obvious.

She said girls can play boys too and that back in Shakespeare's day
it happened all the time.

Mr Kelsey told her she was right and he was happy for her
to be Romeo if she wanted, but that he was also trying to crack
the gender divide we'd naturally formed in our seating choices, so
she'd have to find

a boy willing to be her Juliet.

When Pav volunteered it shocked us all.

'Right. So let's have, Samantha with Matthew. Dominic with
Raidene'.

My fingers are crossed under the table as people start moving seats.

'Kayla and Ferran. Simon with Lana'.

Gutted.

Si is not happy about having to move. Kayla and him switch seats.

I watch Lana as he goes over, trying not to hate him.

Kayla drops her bag on my table and sits down. 'I left my book at
home'.

She looks older than year eight.

Her lips are shiny and she has a necklace half hidden under her
collar.

'What you looking at?' she says. I lift my eyes embarrassed.

'No. I'—

'Okay' says Sir, 'I want you to look at the balcony scene. Read it through. Have some thoughts'.

He writes the page numbers on the board.

Everyone else starts working. I watch Lana finding her page.

Si doesn't look at her once.

'Move up then', says Kayla, shuffling her chair up to mine.

She smells like bubblegum. My body tenses up.

Mr Kelsey sits at his desk with his coffee.

'Are you alright?' Kayla says.

My neck is stiff. 'Yeah. I'm fine'.

She grabs the book out of my hand and starts to find the page.

She's got those white tips painted on her finger nails.

Pav and Jodie are already deep in discussion.

I try to channel my inner Emile and relax.

'I like your nails'.

'What?'

'Nothing', I say, coughing, to cover my tracks.

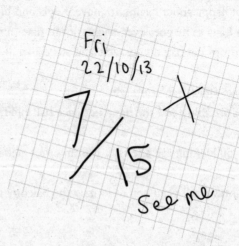

What I Know (I hate describing people)

He has broad shoulders and
a deep voice and
his skin is closer to mine
than Dad's and his watch
is expensive and
he drives an emerald green BMW and
I think he must have like a hundred
of the same cream linen shirt
cos I've never seen him wearing
anything else and he smiles a lot and touches
Mom's shoulders too much and
his name is Michael and
if you opened the catalogue
at the menswear section and
you saw him, staring into the middle distance
in a polo neck
he wouldn't look out of place.

Enjoy The Silence.

Depeche Mode cuts off mid chorus.

This side of town has wider streets and actual front lawns.

The house has deep bay windows and ivy climbing up by the front door. They moved in last week. There's a shower rail sticking up out of the full skip like a giant white radio aerial.

The clouds have cleared.

'So I'm picking you up on Sunday?' says Dad, staring up the street.

'Mom said she'd drop me back'.

'Did she? Would've been nice to let me know'.

I can see movement through the front window.

'Are you gonna say come say hi?'

The look he gives me would burn toast.

'You can send my love'.

I press eject on the tape deck, 'Can I take this?'

He cracks a smile and leans over, fishing in the glove compartment and pulling out an empty case.

'It's only one side so far'. He says.

'That's cool. I have autoreverse'.

'Maybe you could fill side B?'

He looks young in these moments when he's not in control.

'Dad -'

'I'll see you Sunday, big man'.

He loads a different tape into the stereo and starts the engine.

Beenie Man's voice. A drum fill. The stuff Mom never let him play at home.

I open my door. 'Okay, bye'.

Dad cranks it up louder as I get out. The sounds don't fit the street at all.

I feel eyes peering from behind net curtains as I stand on the pavement watching him

drive away.

Fusion.

I have a memory of Nan and Pops coming over for Sunday dinner.
It was sunny and Dad dragged the table
into the back yard and had the speakers
next to the open window.
I remember Emile making Pops laugh with his
low skank and feeling the bass
in the floor when I lay down on the warm slabs.

Mom was really nervous about cooking for Nan.
She was doing curried mutton and rice and peas.
Dad told her she should just make a normal roast dinner, but Mom
insisted. She even made her own greens and coleslaw.
Nan was dressed in her church clothes and brought rum cake.
Pops let Emile have a sip from his bottle of Red Stripe. Dad kept
ducking inside
to change the record.

When Mom brought the plates out she nearly fell over, but managed
to save it and Dad gave her a round of applause.
Everyone's plate had a Yorkshire pudding, filled with the meat and rice.
'Fusion', Mom said, smiling at Nan.
'Just like me!' said Emile.
Pop's and Dad laughed.
I laughed too, gravy dripping down my chin, even though I had no idea
what fusion meant.

Rappers Delight.

I'm stuffed.

Mom let me order the pizzas and it turns out Michael doesn't eat pepperoni.

The three of us at their big round dining table like a poker game.

Instead of two rooms it's one long one, with the sofas and TV down the front end.

Their stereo is expensive Technics Separates.

The bulb has no lampshade yet and I can see it reflected in the dark glass of the patio doors. Anybody outside could see right in.

'I hear you're a hip-hop fan', says Michael, 'I like a bit of Run DMC myself'.

'Cool', I say, hoping he stops. His hands come up. I look at Mom for help.

'I said-a hip, hop, the hippie, the hippie, to the hip hip hop-a you don't stop the rock it to the bang-bang boogie woogie'.

He's proud of himself.

'That's Sugar Hill Gang', I say, 'Not Run DMC'.

Michael's face straightens, 'Right'.

Mom gives me a scowl and holds her forehead.

'You okay?'

'I'm fine. Just a head ache, it'll pass'.

'She's been getting them a lot', says Michael, 'Pregnancy is hard work'.

Mom sips her water and they hold hands. I look away.

'Your room still needs work', she says, 'but the beds good and you've got a TV'.

'My room?'

'Yes, Ferran. Your room. You and Emile each have your own. This is your house too remember'.

She squeezes Michael's hand. I hear Dad kissing his teeth.

'Oh', Mom's holds her stomach, 'Somebody's awake'.

Michael is kneeling down next to her in a flash, leaning in to get close.

'Hello in there, little one. It's Daddy'.

Mom smiles and strokes his head. I feel like I'm intruding.

'You want to say hello, Ferran?'

They both motion me over.

'I'm okay thanks'.

2 Hours Later...

In my new room, in my new bed staring up at my new ceiling,
breathing the new smell.
There are no memories here.
No scratches or stains.
No dirt or bruises or fights.
      I lean down out of bed and fish a pen from my bag.
My headboard has gaps between the wooden beams.
I reach through and write my name onto the wall. The tip scratches
the clean paint.
It looks like a drunk baby wrote it.
I can hear Michael's deep voice through the floor and Mom
giggling as they unpack boxes and I think of Dad,
sitting alone on our back step with a cigarette
looking up at the moon.

Take That.

Kayla's favourite is Robbie
Lana likes Mark.
They both agree the best song is 'Everything Changes'.
Their birthdays are both in September, both like their tea with two
sugars and apparently lots of people think they're sisters.
I learned all of this eavesdropping at break this morning.
It was just me and Pav because Si has conjunctivitis.
At one point Miss Feeney the Food tech teacher came past and told
them off
for doing make up in school. She confiscated Kayla's lip gloss.
Kayla said she couldn't do that because it cost twenty quid. Miss
Feeney told her it would still cost twenty quid when she came and
picked it up at the end of the day.
They whispered all kinds of stuff about Miss Feeney after she'd
gone and at one point
Kayla threatened to punch Shelly.
I'm gonna try and listen to some Take That at some point,
in case it comes in useful.

for the record
I don't think they look like sisters at all.

Waste Paper.

This has to be illegal.

Cello is kneeling over the bin in History. Cage is pointing, ordering him to put his head in it.

We're all watching like it's some twisted circus act.

'Rubbish ideas belong with the rest of the rubbish', says Cage, 'Go on'.

Cello holds the bin either side. People lean forward in their seats.

I'm so angry.

'Stop!'

Cello stops. Everyone turns and stares at me.

'Excuse me, Mr Burke. You have a problem?'

I feel myself starting to sweat.

'It's not good, sir. The germs I mean. He could get sick'.

I look at Cello. His expression is complete defeat.

'It's just waste paper, young man. The perfect place for a head full of rubbish'.

I can't think of anything else to say. Cage grins. 'Perhaps you'd like to join him?'

Si and Pav can't even look at me. Jordan is smiling.

I want to swing my arms and smash them
all away.

For a split second Cello seems to flicker a smile. Then it's gone.

'No, sir', I say, dropping my head.

And the bell goes for lunch.

Être

'Am I boring you, Ferran?'
Miss Zaidel has her hands on her skinny hips in front of
conjugated verbs on the board.
Nous jouons au golf. I didn't mean to yawn out loud.
'No, Miss. Sorry, Miss. Late night'.
'I see. Not up doing revision though, clearly'.
A few people chuckle. I glance at my test paper.
'No, Miss. Sorry'.
Si tries to slide his paper under his textbook next to me, but I've
already seen his mark.
'Well, if I may continue?'
'Yes, Miss'.
'Oui, Madame'
'Yeah, Oui, Madame'.
A few more chuckles. Si smiles, embarrassed.
I stare at the board and let my eyes glaze over, fighting back
another yawn.

TYPES OF TEACHER: A Ferran Burke Lecture

#1: The Mannequin

The Mannequin's soul checked out a while ago, leaving just their body going through the motions.

Common characteristics: Vacant stare. Not hearing questions the first time. Getting people's names mixed up. Lots of wool wear.

#2: The Holiday Rep

The Holiday Rep is just too hyped. Their over enthusiastic approach masks a desperate need to be liked.

Common characteristics: Quoting current pop bands. Making you use their first name. Wearing colourful socks. Sharing 'embarrassing' memories of their own school life in an attempt to bond.

#3: The Drill Sergeant

The Drill Sergeant is basically furious with themselves for ending up as a teacher. Some past decision, mistake or failure has led them to hate their life and their coping strategy is to make everyone else's life even worse.

Common characteristics: Moustache. Constant references to a better/stricter past. An obsession with a highly specific and highly boring subject. Some kind of odour e.g. coffee breath, B.O, musty jacket stink.

#4: The Cool Aunty/Uncle aka The Mayfly

The Mayfly genuinely enjoys their job and cares about their chosen subject. They are interested in dialogue and discussion and welcome questions.

Common characteristics: A scattered, disorganised demeanour. A beat up, but charming car and/or bicycle. Asking for your help carrying things. Some kind of travelling trinket from their backpacking trip to Fiji. A thermos flask that is somehow not lame*.

*Mayfly expected lifespan of max 2-5 years. 99% of those still teaching after this time invariably morph into one of the previous three types.

Sonnet. (- means somebody not speaking on purpose).

Those girls are idiots
Says you
Says anyone with half a brain. All they do is paint each others
faces, giggle and sing stupid songs
You don't even know them
I know them enough, Ferran. Ennit, Pav?
Leave him out of this. Pav, stay out of this. All I was asking is if you
know where they live
Why, you gonna go stalk them? Which one do you fancy?
I don't fancy anyone
Yeah, right. I've seen you staring, ennit, Pav?
Leave him out of it.
You practically dribble all through English. You're always distracted.
Shut up, Si. I'm not kidding.
Oh, Kayla. Kayla, wherefor art thou Kayla?
Kayla?
You love her
—

You should write her a sonnet
Piss off
You're so obvious
You don't know anything. Pav, tell him
Leave him out of this. You're the one in love.
I'm not joking, Si
What you gonna do? Write me a love letter, bore me to death?
Dickhead
Knob. Come on, Pav. We'll miss the bus.
Whatever
Whatever
We still on for town tomorrow?
Course. I'll be at yours before twelve.

Welcome.

It's a girl.
Seven pounds one ounce apparently, which is only about three bags
of sugar.
Emile took the call this morning.
He said Mom sounded tired, but that everything went well and
she'll let us know when they're home.
Luckily Dad's still in bed.
After a short debate, our genius plan is to just not tell him.
He'll find out at some point and that way it won't come from one
of us.
I don't feel great about keeping it secret, but Emile's not gonna say
anything and I really don't want to be the one delivering the news.
'We've got a little sister, man. Crazy'.
'Half sister', said Emile.
He didn't know if they'd chosen a name yet, but he did give me
a ten minute lecture about how and why he'll name his son, Kwame
and his daughter, Ama.
'I reckon they'll go with something more English', I say, spreading
peanut butter on my toast, 'Like Sarah or Sadie or something'
Emile downs the last of the orange juice straight from the carton.
'Based on what?'
'Oh. Nothing. Just a guess'.

Woodwork.

The smell of burning wood.

Sanding my key fob.

It's supposed to be the shape of Jamaica, but looks more like a squashed fish.

Si's is a computer monitor. He's doing the screen with the soldering iron.

Pav is at the big pillar drill, doing his hole. Quiet Michelle is on the next bench.

She's made a small 3D star by slotting two flat stars together.

I look at my fish. Then something bites my neck.

When I turn round, Taylor and Jordan are laughing. Taylor is firing paper clips from an elastic band catapult. He loads up another. I shield my face and take one on the hand.

'Stop it' I say.

Taylor loads another. I grab my planner and use it as a shield.

Taylor switches his aim. Simon yelps as the paper clip hits his ear.

Mr Nelson looks over his newspaper. We all pretend to work.

He disappears again.

Jordan is giggling as he preps more missiles for his captain. Simon turns his blazer collar up.

I look over at Pav, who shakes his head. I turn round anyway.

'Just piss off yeah?'

Taylor smiles and loads up, waiting for me to hide. I don't move.

He takes aim.

I block it just before it hits my face. Jordan and Taylor bump fists.

I look at Simon, huddled over his work. Pav is glaring at me to leave it. Taylor loads up again.

'What's your problem?' I say.

He lowers his aim at my crotch, 'You'. He fires. I dodge and smack my knee on the bench.

Jordan cackles. Mr Nelson looks over his paper again. 'Are you boys finished?'

'No, sir', says Taylor, smiling, 'Ferran was just helping me with something, weren't you, Ferran?'

Jordan giggles behind his hand. I nod to Mr Nelson, 'Yes, Sir. Sand paper, Sir'.

The newspaper goes back up. Taylor gives me two fingers.

Pav is still shaking his head, pissed off that I'm making trouble.

I turn back to my bench and catch quiet Michelle looking at me.

Her 3D star is perfect.

Si holds up his finished computer screen with a sheepish smile.

Then Pav screams.

Dodgem.

We were at the fair in West Smethwick park
on the bumper cars.
I was in Dad's lap helping him steer, Emile was sitting next to us,
shouting orders.
Mom was watching from the side.
Somebody rammed us from behind and I smacked my face on the
steering wheel.
I remember how hot and sticky my nose felt.
As Dad span us round to get the guy back, Mom was waving
and screaming from the side, but he didn't notice.
Emile was staring at me, about to throw up, then I looked down
and
my chest and lap were completely covered
in blood.

Cradle.

It's got to be top three
smells of all time.
So new and fresh, but weirdly familiar, like the smell
of a memory.
I'm deep into the sofa and Mom pushed
a cushion under my elbow so I'm fully supported, but it's still
pretty
nerve wracking.
I'm scared to move in case I drop her.
I can feel her little breaths
even through
the blankets she's wrapped in.
One month old. Little baby Sadie.
Sounds like a song.

Autopilot.

'So he drilled his own hand?'

Mom is on the floor trying to put the little hammock thing together.

The dangly fruit mobile bits are giving her trouble. Michael is at work. Sadie is in my arms.

Joan Armatrading is singing through their posh speakers.

'Yeah. Almost chopped his finger off. It wasn't his fault though'.

'That's awful', she's bending two criss crossed plastic rods more than they're supposed to, there's stains on her t-shirt, 'And he's a good friend?'

'Yeah, why?'

'I've never heard you mention him before'

I picture Pav, slumped over, attached to the pillar drill. He had to have thirteen stitches and only came back to school yesterday.

'Yes!' Mom punches the air as the plastic rods click into place.

Sadie wriggles a bit and whimpers. I rock her slowly til she settles, then catch Mom smiling.

'We'll have you babysitting soon enough'.

'I don't know about that'.

She takes Sadie and lays her into the hammock, checking she's peaceful.

'And how's the rest of school going, I mean, apart from horrific accidents?'

I picture Lana, Taylor, Si and Cage all in a line. 'Yeah, you know'.

'Good boy, you keep it up. Right, I need a coffee. You want some Vimto?'

I can't tell whether I'm relieved or disappointed that she doesn't really care.

'Tea please', I say.

Mom does a double take. 'Tea?'

'Yeah. Two sugars'.

'Look at you. Mr grown up drinks'.

She rubs my hair and goes to the kitchen. I sit on the floor next to the hammock.

Sadie already has a thick patch of black hair. Her skin is just like mine.

I lean close. 'You wanna swap places?'

She makes a tiny beeping sound,

still fast asleep.

Check In.

'I hate these things'.

Ms Martin bangs her keyboard. Her blouse is maroon and cream tie-dye. Everything in the room looks the same.

'They're the future though, right?'

I can hear break time noises from outside. I could be watching Lana eat biscuits.

'I dunno, Miss'.

She hammers the return key with her finger. 'Pretty soon, we'll all have them in every room at home, portable ones too. I saw it on *Tomorrow's World*.

'Right'.

'Where will that leave me?'

She gives up and stares.

'I don't know, Miss'.

'Of course. Ignore me. How are you? How's everything?'

'Fine'.

'Yeah? And at home?'

Her brown hand bag looks like melted chocolate on the desk. I notice she has the same BMW key ring as Michael.

'What do you mean, Miss?'

'I don't know. Any problems? Things that might be a distraction?'

I picture Dad on the back step.

'Don't think so'.

She nods.

'All by yourself now'.

'Miss?'

'Emile. He's not here any more'.

'He was never really here'.

Both of us are surprised. I don't know where that came from. Ms Martin smiles.

'Well aren't you just a box of surprises, Ferran Burke'.

Nag Champa.

The house stinks.

Emile has started burning incense in his room. He says it helps keep him calm when he's studying. Dad said it's fine so long as he puts it out before he goes to sleep.

'So we all have to smell like hippies because it keeps him calm?', I said.

'Your baby brain just can't tune into the benefits, your mind's too shallow'

'Shut up'

'Just open a window', Dad said.

'I'm gonna throw it all in the bin'

'You step one foot in my room and I'll . . .'

He mimes cutting his throat.

'The smell gets into my room, Dad. I tried sleeping with my window open, but Tuna wouldn't stop meowing from outside and kept me awake'.

'She's your cat, Ferran'.

Emile pretends to cry, 'The smell gets in my room, Dad'.

'Oh, fuck you!'

Him and Dad freeze. The shock on their faces.

I walk out before they have chance

to flip their lids.

QUICK NOTE: Take That are AWFUL.

Happy Days.

Morning break.

Biscuits and teas in the busy hall.

Lana and Kayla and them are over by the piano.

Taylor and Jordan and the other goons are trying to impress them with break dancing moves. Jordan spins on his back. Lewis does the worm. The girls laugh like it's a proper show.

'Bullshit', I say, into my cup.

'What is?' Si's flipping a 50p over and over like he's Two Face.

Pav is trying to finish the French homework.

I watch Taylor get down into press up position. Jordan and them start clapping as he goes up and down. Lana and the others seem well into it. Taylor pushes up and claps his hands before dropping into another press up. The goons howl. The girls swoon.

'Who does he think he is, Fonzie?'

Si looks over at them. Taylor does the clap thing again.

'That's really hard to do to be fair'.

'Shut up, Si'

'I'm just saying, he's really strong'.

'Why don't you go ask for his autograph?'

'What's the matter, Ferran, scared Kayla's impressed by muscles?'

'Can we just leave them alone, please?' says, Pav, touching his scar.

I flick a chunk of biscuit at Si and he drops his coin.

Taylor jumps up and takes a bow. The goons all bump fists.

Cello is with them, but on the edge. He doesn't join in like the others.

Jordan and Taylor walk over to the girls. I want to run over and get between them.

I can front flip.

Maybe they'd be into that.

Taylor steals Lana's biscuit and eats it.

She shouts at him, but

she's smiling the whole time.

Arrested Development.

Sadie's crying again.

I don't know what time it is, but it's late.

Mom and Michael are taking it in turns to settle her down.

Her room is next to theirs, down the other end of the landing by
the bathroom.

I can tell who's going by the footsteps.

This time it's Michael.

Emile used to talk about how annoying I was as a baby. How much
I cried.

I always thought he was making it up.

I reach down for my Walkman. The whirring tape.

On my wall, Michael Jordan is flying through the air towards the
basket

as the crowd looks on in disbelief.

The tape clicks. I push my ear buds in and press play.

Crackle, then,

*'Ladies and Gentlemen, there are seven acknowledged wonders of the world,
you are about to witness the eeeeeeiiiiiiiiiiiggggttthhh'*

The tape stops.

      I'm out of batteries.

I hear Michael shuffle back to their room.

I'm wide awake now, so I wrap my duvet round my shoulders and
slide onto the floor.

The cable Michael attached from downstairs means that if I go
to channel six I can watch whatever the downstairs TV was left on.

Volume zero. It's the shopping channel.

Mom has it on in the back ground while we hang out with Sadie.

A man is cutting a shoe in half with a steak knife.
I love these infomercials.
I turn it up a little and listen to the oohs and aahs as the studio
audience marvel at how the knife never loses it's sharpness.
The man is slicing a tomato as thin as paper. It's so cool.
If I get the same amount for Christmas as last year, I could buy
a double set including a free sharpening stone.
The screen goes black, then the word FREEVIEW comes up
in big red letters between lots of capital XXXXXs.
Next thing a woman, wearing just a black bra and knickers
is cleaning a big desk with a feather duster.
She has bright red lipstick and is bending over more
than she needs to.
A phone number is scrolling across the bottom of the
screen in yellow.
If you have a credit card you can call up and pay for full
access.

I've never seen boobs as big before.   They're incredible.
I should switch it off, but I don't.
I turn the volume back down to zero.   Everything is quiet.

The woman is in the kitchen now, baking a cake.
She's still in her underwear.
It's the best thing I've ever seen. I feel nervous and
amazing.
Now there's two women next to a swimming pool.
Their bikinis are too small.

The number scrolls.

The women bounce.

My hand slides into my pyjama bottoms. My skin is tingling. My heart pounding.

Then it stops.

The screen goes black for a second and then the shopping channel starts again.

It's a hoover one.

I close my eyes and imagine the woman's body, bending over with her duster only

her face is Lana's face, still smiling

just for me.

YEAR 9.

where it feels like everyone else is
way ahead of you in
every way.

Playlist.

LOW NOISE HI-FI

90

ULTRA HIGH QUALITY

Stevie Wonder – Too High
Minnie Riperton – Lovin' You
John Coltrane – A Love Supreme, Pt. 2: Resolution
Joni Mitchell – All I Want
DJ SS – The Lighter
Crowded House – Four Seasons In One Day
Rage against the Machine – Know Your Enemy
Charlie Parker – The Bird
The Supremes – Stoned Love
Nirvana – About A Girl (MTV unplugged)
The Gap Band – Outstanding
Nina Simone – My Baby Just Cares For Me

//////AUDIO CASSETTE

I Fight For Me.

If he finds out I've been in here, he'll
kill me,
but it's not right that he gets to keep
all the vinyl.
I woke up with the 'Too High' base line
in my head and I want to blast 'Innervisions' and start
my Sunday properly

It smells like his stupid incense stuff and there's
uni applications and clothes everywhere.
I catch myself in his mirror
my hair cut is fresh, no major spots, am I
getting bigger?
'This year you actually speak to her, understand?'
I nod to myself.
'Swear it'.
'I swear'.

On my way out, I spot the *Rocky IV* video on his shelf.
Mom won't drop him back til later
I've got time to watch it and put it back. It's an Ivan Drago kinda
day.

The case feels light. Something rattles inside.
There's no video.
Just a lighter and what looks like a block of dark
chocolate wrapped tightly
in cling film with a slice
of lemon.

obtuse.

'What's wrong?' says Pav.

I'm between him and Si in Maths, looking at angles.

'Nothing'

Mr Hindle is giving out compasses and protractors. I can see his nose hair from here.

'Are they going out then?'

'Who?'

'Lana and Taylor'

'Who cares?' says Si, rubbing out a pencil line.

'I thought you liked Kayla', says Pav.

We all shut up and take a protractor. 'Thank you, sir'.

Quiet Michelle has her own compass set. Her hair looks different.

Si leans in. 'Everybody's talking about her…', he cups his hands in front of his chest.

'Who, Lana?'

'No. Kayla'.

He lowers his voice. 'Apparently they're massive'.

'Says who?'

'I heard Kelly and Nadia talking about it in form, there's letters and numbers for sizes'.

'Is that why you like her?', says Pav, starting on a kite, 'The boobs?'
'Shut up! I don't like Kayla'.
Quiet Michelle looks over. I pretend to be working.
'I wonder what they feel like', says Si, measuring his triangle.
'Soft', says, Pav.
I screw my pencil into my compass. 'Will you both stop?'
Pav rubs out a line, 'You have to tell us, Ferran. When you squeeze them, tell us what they felt like'.
'What is wrong with you?'
Si nods. 'He's right, Ferran. Promise'.
'I'm not squeezing anything!'
'Not yet, but when you do'.
I check Mr Hindle has his back turned, then I smack them both,

We haven't got a plan,
so nothing can go wrong
        - Spike Milligan

Lips.

I remember a time in the infants, coming home from school
with Emile.
I used to be so jealous that he had his own front door key. He kept
it on a shoelace tied to his back pack.
When we got home, he went straight upstairs to get changed for
football. I went to the kitchen and walked in on Mom and Dad
kissing by the fridge. They were properly going for it and didn't
notice me at first and
I just stood there, watching.
Mom's hands on Dad's face. Dad's hands on her hips. Their bodies
pressed together.
I remember thinking how much attention kissing must take to not
notice me standing right there or even hear the front door.

Catch Up.

Taylor and Jordan were counting
each others pubes in the changing room.
Everyone else was pretending not to look as they got dressed.
Mr Evans was busy trying to fix one of the showers.
Jordan called me a pussy when I wouldn't join in.
'Ferral Ferran's probably bald as an egg'.
Even Si laughed nervously, happy he wasn't the one in their
headlights.
The only one not laughing was Cello, but that's cos he gets
changed in the
corner, out of harms way.
I've got some hair,
but nowhere near as much as those two with their dark
Brillo pads.
They're bigger down there too. Like, nearly men big.
That puberty book Mom got me said the penis is often the last
thing
to develop, which is absolute bullshit.
If God exists, he's a prick, cos having people develop at different
rates is just
asking for trouble, and if we do have to develop
at different rates, why make the penis last?
Let the voice box and the moustache and all the rest of it
catch up later Lord, just sort me out downstairs and stop me
having to get dressed
behind my towel.

Jam.

Minnie Ripperton sings about love.
Dad is on the floor
holding dry wall in place while Patrick nail guns it
to the wooden frame.
It's going to be a studio,
mixing desk and vocal booth and everything.
It'll mean he has a place to run workshops at weekends and
do recording sessions.
Having it out the back of the cafe will be good for business too.
'Artists must eat', Nan said.
          He'd never admit it out loud, but I can tell
Dad is excited.
It feels like the first thing he's really thrown himself into since
Mom left.
I'm supposed to be at Si's with Pav, working on our script for
Drama,

but lately it's like they speak in their own
private language.

Dad gets up and wipes his face. There's white dust in his hair.

'You look like Pop's', I say.

He pretends to lunge for me and I flinch. He smiles, 'Fast like Pops too'.

Patrick pats the wooden frame. 'It's looking good, Theo'.

They shake hands and I think of Lana and Taylor holding hands at break

'Cheer up', laughs Patrick, pointing, 'Might never happen'.

Him and Dad start packing tools away.

'Too late', I say, quiet enough so neither of them
hear.

Greasers.

It's official.
Lana is with Taylor.
They all sit together at break and at lunchtime they either hang out
by the benches next to the sports hall or the girls watch the boys
play football.
It's like that book I read *The Outsiders*.
Taylor and his goons are the Socs and me, Si and Pav are the
greasers, except
we're nothing like the greasers
cos the greasers had their own type
of cool and weren't scared of the Socs.
We just sit to the side talking about quantum leap and staying out
of trouble like pathetic, chicken statues.
         The cliché of it is so lame and I know
it's stupid.
I know that if she's into a prick like Taylor, there must be
something wrong
with her brain.
But that's just it, there's something wrong with
my brain too, because I can't let it go.

In English I watch her
writing Taylor's name in the back
of her exercise book while Si and Pav argue
about similes thinking, if I just had a way to get close
to her, I could show her that I'm cool.

Kayla caught me staring over yesterday.
I thought she was onto me, but then I realised she just thought
I was staring at her chest like everybody
else does.
Being a girl seems hard.
Being a girl with big boobs looks exhausting.

Lunges.

'Did you hear that? She said, Mama!'
Mom has Sadie on her knee like a ventriloquist's dummy.
All I heard was a string of random syllables.
'Yeah', I say, 'Definitely'. 'Clever girl', Mom snuggles Sadie's neck.
Sadie cackles. It's hard not to laugh along. Joni Mitchell is singing
about jealousy.
Emile comes in and sprawls himself across a chair like he lives here.
Mom presses her forehead.
'You okay, Mom?' 'I'm fine, love. Just a head ache. It'll pass', she
throws a cushion at Emile, 'Have you got all the
prospectuses?'
Emile groans.
I sense another university conversation coming so I go to the
kitchen and click on the kettle.
Michael comes through the back door in his tracksuit and sweat bands.
There's dark patches round his armpits.
'Morning, Ferran'.
'Hi Michael'.
He frowns.
'Mike, sorry'.
He checks his watch and nods, then gets a glass of water.
We got here a couple of hours ago and he was already out running then.
I've never seen Dad run anywhere.
'Best way to start the day', he says, lunging by the sink.
I don't tell him I can think of at least four hundred better ways if
he'd like
me to list them.

Collision.

I'm power walking to Physics in case any teachers catch me
running.
As I come round the corner by form,
I smack right into someone and go flying.
I catch my breath and look up and Cello is standing there, rubbing
his head.
I get up.
'Sorry, man. You okay?'
'Yeah'.
'Are you late too?'
'Did the bell go?'
I pick up my bag. 'Ages ago. Where you going?'
'Toilet'.
'What about lesson?'
Cello shrugs.
'Okay', I say, 'See ya'.
'Yeah', he says.
As I power walk away
I look back and he's just standing there, by the wall
watching me go.

Air Tonight.

Si got a mini fridge for his birthday.
It's big enough to hold eight cans of Tab Clear. We've had one
each already.
I'm doing press ups while him and Pav debate the best way
to package tennis balls for our maths homework.
I can do ten now without stopping, but still can't do the clap thing.
'Trust me, Si, a hexagonal prism cuts the dead space'.
'It looks like it does, but it'd be less with a triangular, look'.
'You're wrong'.
'I'm not. Ferran, tell him'.
'Let's go park', I say.
The pair of them look at each other.
'What for?' says Pav.
'I dunno. Fresh air? To hang out?'
They go right back to debating like I'm not there.
I crawl over to Si's boom box and load up his Crowded House CD.
The twang of a guitar riff.
Si waves a finger, 'Turn it off, Ferran. We need to work'.
'Music helps. Stimulates brain cells. Right, Pav?'
Pav shakes his head. 'We'd figure this out quicker if you helped us'.
'What's to figure out?', I say, 'It's just maths. Who cares?'
The pair of them give me the exact same look that Dad gave
Mom that one Christmas dinner when Granddad Phillip said
that Phil Collins was the best musician
this country ever produced.

Drowned.

Cross country is the worst, but cross country
on a wet and windy November morning
is a whole extra level of shit.
My t-shirt is stuck to me and my knees feel like they're gonna fall off.
Si and Pav are taking it in turns to jog in each other's slip stream.
We're near the back because nether of them is very fast and
I don't want to run by myself.
The only people behind us are fat Bryan and Liam Dakin who always walks
the whole circuit in protest.
By the time we get back to the changing rooms, most people are already
showered and getting dressed.
Jordan starts a round of applause as we walk in.
'Look at the wet pussies'
People laugh. Si and Pav turn their backs and start to get changed.
I can't feel my fingers as I try to peel off my t-shirt. Jordan's not done.
'You going for the shittest times ever recorded?'
More laughing. Si and Pav look nervous.
'Piss off, Jordan'. I drop my wet top on the floor.
There's a few groans. Si closes his eyes as the goons pipe in, egging
Jordan on.
'Nah'.
'You gonna let him say that to you J?'
Jordan comes over.

Si and Pav shuffle down the bench separating themselves from me.

'What d'you say?'

I never understand that question.

He heard what I said. Everyone did.

I turn to face him. We're pretty much the same height now.

'Whatever', I say, which I've found is usually the best response to make

it look like you're not chickening out, but also not fan the flames.

Not today though.

He pushes me in the chest and I fall back onto the bench, narrowly missing

the blazer hooks on the wall.

A few more laughs.

Jordan bows to the crowd as I stand up.

He puffs his chest. 'What? You wanna go?'

My frozen fingers ball into fists. I'd love to smack him.

He's not muscley like Taylor. If I jumped on him, I reckon I could have a go.

Then Mr Evans walks in with Bryan and Liam looking like cats who've had a bath.

'Chop chop, boys', he says, 'No time for showers now. The bell's going any second'.

My fingers are still numb as I pull off my socks.

Si and Pav are looking at me like disappointed parents.

Taylor is doing his hair in the mirror and, over in the corner,

Cello is sitting quietly with his bag on his lap,

watching me.

Dear Lana

You'll ~~never~~ see this, so it's okay. I just wanted to say
that I think you're ~~beautiful~~
                        cool
and if we could hang out or something for a bit
you might ~~think I'm okay too. To be honest~~
I have ~~absolutly no~~ idea why this because
I'm ~~never~~ ever going to give it to you and the
only person who ~~will ever see it~~ is the bin.

~~Idiot~~ ~~Idiot Idiot~~ Idiot
                              CHICKEN!!!!

Smoke.

Dad's on the back step with a cigarette.
Any time he's home and there's no music playing I know it's bad.
Drowning out your sorrows with Coltrane is one thing

not even wanting to

is way worse.

I lean on the fridge.
The doorway frames him like a painting
'Dad?'
He takes a long drag, blowing smoke upwards.
'She's marrying him'.
There's an official looking letter open on the table, solicitors logo
and typed writing.
'When?'
'No idea. I have to sign those'.
I want to get closer to him. Go over and offer a hug.
I tell myself if he looks at me I will.
If he looks at me, I'll walk over and give him the best hug anyone's
ever given.
He doesn't turn around.
I watch him smoke and feel helpless.
'I'll put some music on', I say,
putting my bag down and leaving him
alone.

Industry.

Dad had a record deal.
Him and his best friend from art college had a production duo called
Blue Marcus. Dad played bass and the drum machine, his friend played keys.
They'd get different vocalists to perform with them.
Some A&R from a major label saw them at a gig and signed them.
Dad and Mom had already met. She was at the same college studying photography
and used to take pictures of rehearsals and sets.
Dad and his friend dropped out of their final year to go touring.
Mom went with them and by the time they came home,
she was pregnant with Emile.
They lived with Nan and Pops for a bit until Dad's advance money came in and
he used it for the down payment on their own house (the one we still live in).

While they were working on new tracks the label suggested adding a permanent female singer to make them more marketable.

Dad's friend said it was for the best. Dad went along with it.

Blue Marcus put out a single that got into the charts.

Everything was going great.

Emile was born and Dad was getting ready
to record the album.

Then the label told him he was dropped.

They were going with his friend and the singer as a duo.

The contract Dad had already signed made him powerless to do anything about it.

His friend wouldn't return his calls.

Dad went to his friends house, smashed up his car and got arrested.

The singer went on to become half famous. His ex friend moved to America and became a successful behind the scenes record producer.

Dad eventually went back to college and trained as a sound engineer.

He never got on stage again.

Superman.

'I can't believe they did it', says Si.

We're in town outside Nostalgia & Comics huddled round his Superman #75.

'Doomsday is insane', he says, 'You should both have got this too. They actually killed him! This will be worth loads one day'.

'It's a gimmick', says Pav, 'Nobody cares about Superman anymore'. He takes out his *Dark Knight Returns*, 'This is the real shit. Frank Miller is the Don'.

'Says who, your sister? How much you pay for that?'

They start arguing again.

I'm the only one without a bag. I'm still saving for the neon Air max 95s.

I look up the street at the huge cylinder of the Rotunda. The bright red of the Coca Cola sign against the grey sky.

'We should get to the bus stop', I say, 'It's getting late'.

Si carefully slides his comic into its bag. 'What's wrong? Scared of the dark?'

'Shut up, Simon. This is town, remember'.

'I'm not scared', he says.

'He's right, Si', says Pav, 'I told my mom I'd be back before six'.

'Jesus. Am I babysitting?'

We walk up towards the island and I think about Sadie, giggling in my arms.

'Shit'.

Pav speaks for us all as a gang of older boys come round the corner.

Dark army coats. Doc Martins. My stomach drops.

Pav looks at me, 'Do we run?'

They're getting closer.

'Fully', I say, 'Split up, fast as you can, get to McDonald's okay? Si?'

Si is just grinning. 'You're such babies'.

I grab his arm. 'Don't mess around. Look at them! Let's go'.

I'm about to run when he calls out. 'Darren!'

The leader of the pack squints at us. 'Little Si?'

'Yeah! It's me!'.

He knows them. Or one of them at least.

I still don't like it.

I look at Pav. He's bricking it too, but we can't run now.

They look like a rubbish version of Nirvana.

Darren has an undercut and a nose ring. He looks at me and Pav like we're dog shit.

'What ya doin?' His voice is proper Wolverhampton.

'Ah, nothing much, just hanging', says Si, 'What you dudes up to?'

I can't help but cringe. Darren looks at his mates and grins. 'Ow's ya sister?'

'Yeah, yeah she's cool. She's in Manchester now'.

'Manchester? That's a lung way to go for a shag'. The other boys laugh. Darren grins and humps the air. My stomach tightens. Si squirms and tries to laugh it off.

Darren looks at me and Pav. 'Scraping the barrel for mates ay ya?'

He leans towards Pav and sniffs. 'Anybody else smell curry?'

The words are a knife. I look across. Pav's about to cry. Si doesn't do anything.

'Fuck you'. I say under my breath.

'You say somethin, Daley Thompson?', He steps to me, 'Look lads, it's little Daley fucking Thompson'. And I could boot him in the balls. Full whack. Make him sorry.

'Lamp him, Daz', says one of them. Darren puffs up his chest.

'Want it do ya, mutt?'

As he raises his fist I think of Emile.

'Y'alright boy?'

It's a thick set man with dreads and a sheepskin jacket.

Darren's chest deflates and he backs up.

The man stands firm and stares them all out. They suddenly all look like skittles

waiting to be knocked over.

'Fock this', says Darren, 'Come on lads. Tell Lucy to phone me if she's lonely, Si',

He grins at me before turning away.

Relief washes over me. Then embarrassment.

The man with the dreads waits until the gang go around the corner.

'All good?'

I nod.

'Thank you', says Pav.

The man nods and moves on. Me and Pav look at each other.

Neither of us looks at Si.

We just start walking.

English Friends.

Si's house is nothing like ours.
Everything is neat and quiet and
put away in cupboards.
It smells of furniture polish instead of food.

There's always Sunny Delight in the fridge and
the way he talks to his mom,
if I spoke to Mom
like that
I'd lose my teeth.

Andrex.

I'm late.
Emile didn't make his usual racket
leaving this morning and my alarm is rubbish.
I fix my tie and get my cutest face ready before walking into
reception.
Denise at the desk loved Emile and I'm gonna need to channel
whatever charm genes
we possibly share to avoid having to sign in and get a detention.
'I'm so sorry, I was helping Emile find his textbook. He's got a big
test today. He said to say hi. I love your nails'.
It works.
I bop down the empty corridor. Maybe there's more than one
smooth Burke.
It's only Geography first lesson and Mr Macklin won't say
anything.

They're sitting in one of the cloakroom booths, amongst the coats.
Kayla has her arm round Lana, who's crying and I should just keep
walking, but I stop.
'Get lost, Boffin' says Kayla.
'You okay?'
'We're fine. Jog on'.
Lana looks at me. Her cheeks are blotchy and she's holding a clump
of loo roll. I smile at her.
'Can I help?'
Kayla scowls. 'You can piss off'.
They whisper to each other as I walk on.

'Oi, Boffin, hold on'.

'My name's Ferran, Kayla'.

'Whatever, come here'.

I walk into the booth.

'Wait here with her while I run to the upstairs toilets'.

'What for?'

'Shut up. Just wait with her, okay?'

She squeezes Lana's shoulder, 'I'll be right back, they'll have some in the other loos'.

Lana nods and wipes her nose, looking at me.

Kayla squares up to me with her woman's body, 'If any teacher's come, make something up'.

'What happened?'

She glances back at Lana. 'Girl stuff'. She whacks my arm.

'Ow'

'A little taster. Mess this up and you'll get way worse, trust me'.

She checks the corridor and bounces off.

I have butterflies as I sit down opposite Lana. This is the first time I've ever

been alone with her. It feels like a chance to connect, but she's upset and I'm being selfish.

I offer a smile. 'You look like the Andrex puppy'.

Lana frowns, 'I look like a dog?'

'No. I meant, with all the loo roll, the little one, from the advert, the cute one'.

I look down. Idiot. Idiot.

When I look up, she's smiling.

'I'd take being a puppy right now'.

I smile back, feeling amazing. 'Is there anything I can do?'

'I don't think so. Unless you can control the moon'.

'The moon?'

'Cycles. Like the tides? Doesn't matter'.

She blows her nose, like properly, and somehow it's not disgusting at all.

'Sorry', I say, 'I can't even control myself'.

She laughs a little bit. 'You're in English with us, right?'

'Yeah. And Tech. And Drama last year'

'Yeah. You're on the clever clever table'.

'Nah, I'm'–

'How come you're not in lesson?'

'I'm late. No big deal. I do it all the time. Whatever'.

'Right'.

'I'm not a boffin. At all'.

'Okay'.

She folds up her toilet roll. 'Thanks for staying with me, Ferran'.

'No problem. Any time'.

'Got some'.

Kayla is waving a little purple box.

She moves it behind her back when she sees me looking.

'Come on', she says to Lana, 'I think Miss Lacey saw me'.

Lana gets up. I stand too. Kayla points at me, 'Tell anyone about this, you're dead. Understand me?'

I nod. She looks me up and down. 'You're kinda cute. For a boffin'.

I don't know where to look. I feel like one of those fairground teddy bears.

Lana smiles. 'He's not a boffin. At all'.

'Whatever', and she leads Lana away.

I sit down and lean back, letting the coats swallow me up.

Maybe I'll forget all my lessons today and just sit here

glowing, until it's time

to go home.

Give Way.

Emile passed his driving test.
First time.
Unusually for him, he didn't even try and play it down.
He was blasting jungle
when I got back from Mom's and danced into the kitchen when he came downstairs,
sticking his test paper to the fridge.
One minor fault for signalling late.
'Do you know what this means, little brother?'
'A car?'
He grabbed my shoulders and shook me like a doll.
'Freedom!'

Glimpse.

Me and Pav are walking to Chemistry.
Outside the Science block, behind the big bins, Kayla's friend
Shelly has got
quiet Michelle pinned against the wall, while another girl
goes through her bag.
As we get closer, they pretend
they're just talking. Michelle's face is flushed.
My jaw tightens. 'What you doing?'
'Nothing', says Shelly flashing me evils.
The other girl drops Michelle's bag, spilling her books, and they
walk off laughing.
Michelle bends down to pick up her things.
I look at Pav. Pav shrugs. And
before I can go over and help, Michelle is already
gone.

Trenches.

Cello's gonna cry.

His lips are clamped shut trying to hold it back.

Cage has him out in front of the whole class and is holding up his essay.

We had to write about life on the Allied front line in World War I.

I was pretty chuffed when I saw my 71%.

Cello got his wars mixed up and mentioned Hitler.

Cage read it out, putting on a pathetic voice to mock him.

Most of the class laughed along, relieved it isn't them standing out front.

I didn't laugh. This isn't right.

Cello clearly tried hard with it, he just made a mistake.

'I'm surprised you didn't put astronauts in there for good measure', says Cage

A few chuckles.

Cello's hands go into his pockets.

I know he's squeezing fists in there.　　　　I'm doing the same.

Si and Pav are fidgeting next to me.

Cage holds the essay out in front of him

like it's litter he had to pick up.

'I'm not sure what to do with this, Mr Tardelli. What do you think?'

Cello shrugs.

The whole room gasps as Cage rips it in half.

The sound of it tearing is like a scratch on my heart.

'There's only one place this belongs', says Cage scrunching up the pieces.

Cello is looking at Jordan, sitting over on the right. Jordan is just staring.

Cage drops the scraps into the bin and brushes his hands.

And Cello is crying.

No sounds, but tears are running down his face.

I fucking hate this man.

People like him never get told.

I stand up.

Pav mouths, 'What are you doing?'

I don't know what I'm doing, but I'm doing it.

'Something wrong, Mr Burke?' Cage glares at me.

I look at Cello, wiping his face.

'That's not right'.

'You have a problem with what I did?'

Si is wide eyed, shaking his head. Pav looks like he's about to hyperventilate.

I hold eye contact with Cage 'Yes, sir. You're out of order, ripping up his work'.

Everyone is looking at me now. My legs are shaking. Cage seems almost intrigued.

'Is that right?'

'He just made a mistake. Anyone could've done it. It's not fair'.

'I see. And is there something you plan to do about it?'

I pick up my essay.

Cage smiles like a shark.

I think of Emile. *Maybe it's you, Ferran.*

Then I kiss my teeth and

tear it in half.

Fuel.

I had a fight with Craig Law in year six.

He was telling people that Emile got caught stealing from his mom's shop.

I told him to shut up.

He said his mom was gonna call the police, but she's too kind.

I said his mom was a liar.

He said, don't speak about my mom.

I said, don't speak about my brother.

He said his mom said Jamaican's are all criminals.

I jumped on him.

Mom and Dad were at work, so Nan had to come pick me up from Mr Hogan's office.

I sat there while he explained to her how my behaviour was unacceptable.

Nan nodded in agreement.

My shoulder hurt from hitting the floor and my hand hurt from hitting Craig.

When we got to the end of the street, Nan asked me what Craig said.

I told her.

She took us to Kentucky Fried Chicken and bought us Zinger burgers.

I said I was sorry.

Nan told me to always keep my strength up.

She said there are plenty of Craigs.

Charged.

'Drama, French, Geography, I.T', says Pav, 'Easy'.

Si nods. 'Same. Exactly. Ferran?'

I look at the handout.

The school logo and the words: *'Where do you want to go? Who do you want to be?'*

This morning we had an assembly about GCSEs and the different subject choices for options.

They're still giving me grief about what happened in History yesterday.

How stupid I am.

How it had nothing to do with me. How I'm only making things worse for us.

I have my first detention later and they're genuinely disgusted.

And I don't care.

Maybe it was stupid. Maybe I'm an idiot. I don't know.

What I do know is that I felt more alive yesterday than I've felt in ages.

They don't get it.   They don't get me.

'You done, Ferran?' says Si.

I look at the handout again.

Who do you want to be?

'Yeah', I say,

'I'm done'.

YEAR 9 OPTIONS FORM – YOUR CHOICES

Student Name: **Form:**

Parental Signature: **Date:**

Compulsory CORE SUBJECTS (Everyone studies these)

English Language **English Literature** **Maths**

Science **Core PE**

All subjects are GCSE unless stated otherwise

CORE +
(Tick one of these boxes)

French	
Spanish	
History	
Geography	

Remember you can choose more than one of these by ticking one or more of the options in the **Additional Subjects** box.

ADDITIONAL SUBJECTS (Tick three of these boxes)
Please not you are not able to select both Art & Design and Textiles

Art & Design		BTEC ICT	
BTEC Enterprise (Business)		Media Studies	
Computer Science		Music Performance	
Drama		Photography	
Food Tech		Physical Education	
BTECH Hospitality and Catering		Religeous Studies	
French		Design & Tech	
Geography		Sociology	
BTECH Health & Social Care		Spanish	
History		Textiles	

Please also select a reserve choice in the box below

Reserve:

WAKENS TIP

Pretty Dumb.

It's just the two of us   three seats apart
        waiting for Cage to show up and go crazy.
        Cello is scribbling on his battered work planner. Rings and
rings of biro as black as his hair. His fingers are thin and his nails
    are chewed. He was already sitting here when I walked in.
                    He hasn't said a word.
    We're half way through year nine, but this is my first ever
                        detention.
            I'm not even sure how long they last.
        A block of sunlight covers Cage's empty desk.
    A neat stack of exercise books. A pot full of the same pen.
    There's dates in neat chalk on the black board and that World
War I recruitment poster with the guy in the top hat saying YOU
                    pointing right at us.
There's a breeze from the open window and I can hear the sounds
        of everyone else in the playground heading home.
    I'm scared, but my fear is muddied with something else.
                    Something good.
    I take out my planner too. It looks brand new. I can't think of
                anything cool to doodle.
Lana pops into my head. We could see them doing hockey from
                Biology this afternoon.
        Her bouncing pony tail. Those long socks.
                'You're pretty dumb'.
            His voice is deeper than I'd noticed.
            He doesn't look up. Keeps scribbling.
        'Yeah', I say, starting to scribble too.

135

'He's gonna have it in for you too now'.
His pen scratches the page. Mine does the same
'Yeah'.
The sun slips away and the desk goes dark and as the door starts to
open
just before Cage walks in
me and Cello look at each other and
we smile.

Gemma's Metaphor.

I'm watching *Gladiators*.
Shadow is getting ready to smack Andy from Bristol off his pillar.
The front door slams and Emile comes in carrying a mini cactus.
Tuna looks up from the sofa. It looks like a spiky green thumb in a pot.
He smells like Hugo Boss. He aced his mock exams and, now he can borrow the car,
has been out every day since we broke up for the holidays.
'Is that real?'
'How the hell do I know?', he says, handing it to me, 'Just put it somewhere will ya, I've gotta get changed. Where's Dad?'.
'At the cafe. Patrick's dropping him home. Where's the tree?'
'Oh. They didn't have any left'.
'Did you even go?'
'Yes!'
'We need a tree, Emile. He gave you the money'.
'I know. Jesus, who are you the secret police?'
He runs upstairs and I'm left with the plant. Tuna goes back to sleep.
A sweaty and flustered Andy is being interviewed by Ulrika. 'Yeah, he's a big guy, and I just, I don't know, I tried, Susie I tried! Daddy loves you!'
The crowd applaud as the camera cuts to a little girl waving her big foam glad hand.
I press at the dark soil in the pot. The cactus is real.
Emile comes back down in a different shirt and more after shave.
'Okay, I'm gone'.

'Where?'

He jingles the car keys. 'Town. I'm meeting Stacey'

'We need a tree', I point at the old box of battered tinsel and baubles in the empty corner.

'I know. I'm on it'.

'When?'

'Just chill out will ya'.

'Hold on, who's Stacey?'

Emile smiles. 'A friend'.

'So who's this from?'

'Gemma. Keep up little bro'.

'And what am I supposed to do with it?'

'I dunno. She says it's a metaphor for our relationship, so keep it alive, yeah? I like her'.

'More than Stacey?'

He checks his watch. 'Shit. Tell Dad I've got my key and I'll sort the tree tomorrow. How do I look?'.

'Like someone who doesn't deserve plants'.

'Good one, shit face'.

Another smile and he's gone.

When the adverts come on I take the cactus to the kitchen, give it some water and sit it in a saucer by the window.

The spikes look like silver fur. I resist the temptation to stroke it.

'I'll keep you alive, Gemma's metaphor'.

Then I grab a packet of Skips and go back to the telly.

Three Kings.

It's like chewing a pillow.

Dad got distracted playing records and left the turkey in the oven.

The mashed potatoes are lumpy, the gravy is brown water,

there's no stuffing and the carrots are still rock hard.

Emile got an amp for his semi acoustic.

I got new headphones and a Charlie Parker anthology on vinyl.

Bird is blowing right now from the living room.

Nan is in Jamaica til new years, making arrangements for when she moves home

in the summer, so it's just the three of us, sat round the table in paper crowns.

Emile gives up. 'I'm kinda full, Dad'

'You've hardly touched it'

My jaw aches. Mom is picking us up later to stay with her until new years.

Dad pokes at his carrots, 'It's terrible isn't it?'

'No. No. I'm just, not that hungry. It's great, isn't it Ferran?'

They both look at me. I force myself to swallow. 'It's the worst meal I've ever had'.

Emile scowls.

Dad puts his cutlery down.

And laughs.

It feels like somebody popped a balloon.

'How can a bird taste like wood?' He says, wiping his eyes.

Emile holds up his turkey leg, 'Wood pigeon'.

We laugh more and I feel older.

Like I've stepped up a level.

Dad drops his napkin onto his plate and sighs. 'Bwoi, At leas mi never mek di cake'.

He holds out his hands and we both take one.

'My boys', he says, squeezing us,

'My men'.

Cold Call.

I don't know what I'm doing.

Sitting next to the phone, phonebook in my lap, scrolling through the Js looking for Jacobs.

I don't know her address and there's no way I'm calling her. I'm just messing around.

There's four Jacobs numbers.

I don't recognise the street names, but one of them is a B67 postcode. That could be her.

Or they could be ex-directory and that's some other random Jacobs family and I just breathe down the line and hang up like some thirteen year old stalker.

But I want to call. I want to do something. I'm sick of being so passive.

I pick up the receiver. 0121 429

I hang up.

What am I thinking? *Hi Lana, it's Ferran from school. I kept you company when you were crying in the cloakroom, remember? I just wanted to check you were okay. Oh and what's the deal with you and that dickhead Taylor? Okay then. Bye.*

I shut the phonebook.

Idiot.

Then I open it up again, tear out the page and fold it small enough to fit

in my pocket.

Frosting.

Jordan is with Kayla and Taylor is with Lana.
Shelly went with Lewis and everyone else was in a two already
which just left me
and quiet Michelle.
At the book shelves, Si and Pav are already excitedly discussing
a multi layered spaceship cake with silver icing. They smile
awkwardly as I get closer.
'Sorry, man', says Pav, 'Shall we ask if we can be a three?'
'No worries', I say, grabbing the two books nearest to me, 'I'm
good'.

Michelle has already covered half a piece of A3 paper
with notes and ideas.
'Wow. You don't mess around, eh?'
She shrugs, embarrassed.
'No. I mean, it's good. Good work'.
She's blushing. Her eye lashes are super long.
'If we're going Chinese, we might have to make buns or pancakes?'
'What?'
She points at the books. One of them is called *Dim Sum for Beginners*,
the other *Vegan Dreams*.
'Oh. Sorry. I didn't notice'
I look over at Taylor and Lana, he's twisting her hair while she
flicks through the pages.
Jordan and Kayla are playing slaps.
'Remember, the best food, is food that matters!' says Miss Feeney
from her desk, 'Anybody can make a cake, I want you to tell me a

story'.

'What does that even mean?'

Michelle leans in and her elbow touches mine. She pulls it away quickly and sits up.

'I think she means that we choose something we care about. What's your favourite cake?'

'I dunno. My nan makes one with rum and ginger which is really good'.

'Okay'

'Yeah, but we can't bring rum to school, unless you want to get drunk?'

I wait for her to laugh. She doesn't.

'Any others?'

'Not really, unless bun and cheese counts?'

'What's bun and cheese?'

'It's a cake, kind of. A bun. With raisins and you slice it with butter and cheese. It's Jamaican I guess'.

'Cool. Can you get a recipe? '.

'I dunno. What's your favourite cake?'

Her face goes full serious. 'If I had to choose, I'd say either a classic New York cheesecake, or carrot, but only if there's mascarpone frosting and pecans'.

'Right', I say, 'Mascarpone. Doesn't he play for AC Milan?'

'It's a cheese'.

'Yeah. Course, I know. I like carrot cake. Shall we do that? Does carrot cake matter enough?'

'The right carrot cake does', she says, pulling another piece of paper from the pile.

I look back at Pav and Si, reading from the same book.

'You're a comic fan, right?'

Michelle stops writing.

'I mean, I remember I saw you once, in town, ages ago, in Waterstones. By the comics'.

'Manga', she says, sternly.

'Yeah, Manga, comics, same thing'.

She stares at me blankly.

'It's really not'.

Free World.

It's like sadness on a plate.

The burgers are balsa wood dry and the chips are soggy.

Year tens and elevens are allowed to go off site for lunch and it's no surprise that almost all of them do, which means we're the oldest ones in the busy lunch hall.

Si and Pav don't seem to mind the crappy food as they laugh about last nights episode of *Bottom*.

'I can't believe you missed it, Ferran. It was hilarious!'

They laugh again. I don't even like the show. It's just two idiots beating each other up and drinking aftershave, but these two think it's amazing.

'Did you get another detention?' says Pav.

'Yeah. French'.

'He didn't do the homework', says Si.

'No big deal. You just sit there for half an hour. It's fine'.

'It's stupid', he says. Pav agrees.

Taylor, Lana and Jordan and the others are on the table over by the windows making each others tie knots as fat as they can be without falling apart. Cello is sitting at the edges like usual.

On the far table where the packed lunch people eat, I can see Michelle sitting by herself.

I stand up.

'Where you going?' says Si.

'I'll see you later'.

30 Seconds Later . . .

'Hi'

'What's wrong?' She's looking at me like I'm lost.

'Nothing. Can I sit down?'

'You're already sitting down'.

'Yeah. That cool?'

'Free world'.

The kids who sit at this table are almost all top setters.

Every lunch box I can see has cool looking stuff inside; thick crusty bread sandwiches, fruit salads. Michelle is eating some kind of pasta with little bits of what looks like sausage.

I look at my plate.

'School dinners are lame'.

'School is lame', she says.

And it's the truest line I've heard in ages.

Factoring Quadratics (A)

Factor each expression

$$ax^2 + bx + c = 0$$
$$a, b, c = \text{known numbers}, a \neq 0$$
$$x = \text{the unknown}$$

1. $-2x^2 - 13x + 7$
2. $2x^2 - 21x + 27$
3. $x^2 - x - 20$

a = confusion
b = frustration
c = pointlessness
x = boredom

Long Way.

'Ferran, wait up!'

We're heading to Geography first lesson. Si and Pav are walking ahead. They look back annoyed as Cello catches up.

'What's up?' he says, slightly out of breath. He's got toothpaste on his chin.

'Not much. You?'

'Not much'.

'What's up is, we're gonna be late', says Si.

'What lesson you got?' I say.

Cello has to think. 'French'.

Si rolls his eyes, 'French is that way. We're going this way'. He starts to walk off. Pav looks at me then follows him.

'Yeah, right', says Cello, 'See you later then'. He heads off in the direction he came from.

I watch Si and Pav getting further away.

'Hey, wait up!'

Cello looks surprised as I catch him up.

'I'll walk the long way round. Geography is dead'.

He smiles. 'Not as dead as French'.

And we walk together towards reception.

Team Carrot.

It tastes like heaven.

Dark and sweet and just moist enough. There's a slight crust to the outside then the almost fluffy middle and the frosting? Man. It's perfect.

'Wow' I say, taking another bite.

Michelle isn't eating hers. She's just watching me, smiling. I look around at everyone else.

Si and Pav's spaceship cake looks like it crashed. Kayla is shouting at Jordan because he forgot to add their flour. Lana and Taylor burned their biscuits.

I feel like I'm in on a secret that only me and Michelle know. This was easily the most fun I've had in a lesson ever.

'You're good', I say.

'We both made it'.

'All I did was bring flour and carrots and stir like you told me'.

'Fold. You folded, not stirred'.

'Exactly, see, I don't even know what I was doing. This is your cake'.

Miss Feeney comes over.

'How did it turn out?'

I'm beaming. 'See for yourself, Miss'.

Michelle cuts her a piece. Miss takes a bite, then closes her eyes.

'Goodness me', she says, 'This is special. The pecans are great and, do I taste a hint of cherry?'

Michelle nods. 'Sour cherries. We cut them up really fine'.

Miss takes another bite and makes happy eating noises. 'Well done you two'.

'Actually, Miss, all I really did'–

'It was a team effort, Miss'.

'Well, if this is what you produce together, you're quite a team. I look forward to what you make next'.

Michelle holds up her hand for the high-5 and, as I slap her palm, I swear I see Lana watching.

Hash.

I'm stirring the corned beef in the pan.

Tuna is going crazy attacking sound proofing foam on the kitchen floor.

It's left overs from Dad's studio behind the cafe.

Now it's finished he can run sessions and work with artists. He hasn't done any yet.

'You can't rush these things', he says.

'Have you even told anyone it's there?' says Emile pouring ginger beer into glasses.

'All in good time', says Dad.

Emile shakes his head like Mom used to.

'You could put posters up at the college', I say spooning rice onto plates. I copied Patrick's trick with the tea towel under the pot lid to steam it and get it fluffy and it worked, 'I bet there's loads of people who'd come'.

Dad gives me the look that says, leave it, so I do.

Emile brings cutlery as I lay hash over the rice. Dad takes the hot pepper sauce from the side.

'I already put some in', I say, 'Maybe have a taste first'.

Dad smiles and splashes sauce across his mound of food.

We all eat quietly. Tuna is taking a breather, buried in the foam.

The beef is just spicy enough.

Emile: Did you put potato in this?

Me: Yep. Little ones, for texture. I crisped them up with the onions first.

Dad: It really works.

Me: Thanks

Emile: 'Little Rustie Lee eh?'

Dad laughs.

Me: Shut up.

Dad: He's just jealous cos me and him can't boil an egg. You're the chef.

Emile: I can boil an egg.

Dad grins at me.

Emile: I've made boiled egg loads of times.

Dad: Good for you, son. That's brilliant.

He laughs. I join in. Emile scowls for as long as he can hold it then laughs as well.

And Your Mom.

MATE. YOUR HOUSE IS SO DIRTY YOUR VACOOM
          HAS MUD FLAPS

Well your house is so dirty you wipe your arse
    before you take a shit

Your so ugly Hello Kitty said goodbye

CAN YOU
SPELL?!

The Elephant Man called, he wants his face back

Your house is so small you have to go outside
            to   change   your   mind

I heard FREDDY KRUGER HAS nightmares aBout Your mom

YOUR FAMILY TREE IS A CACTUS
    EVERYONE ON IT IS A
            PRICK

Pea Man.

Friday night.

Michael's made risotto.

I've never had it before and when he put the plate in front of me I thought it was just sloppy rice, but it's delicious.

Creamy and sweet with the earthy mushrooms and little crispy onions on top.

'The peas are what makes it', he says, as me and Mom tuck in, 'Mushrooms get the glory, but people underestimate the pea'.

I laugh. Michael looks offended.

'I'm sorry, that was, I thought that was a funny line. Like a super hero catchphrase or something. *Don't underestimate Pea Man*'.

There's an awkward moment, then Michael laughs too.

'Pea man. That's very good'.

Sadie is in her little pen thing, babbling away. Mom pours more wine.

'So, what's happening at school?'

'Not much'.

Michael tears himself more garlic bread, 'You must be coming up to GCSE options time, no?'

Mom looks at him, surprised.

'Tabitha is year nine too. George's daughter?'

'Right', says Mom, drinking.

Michael spoons rice onto his bread, 'So have you already decided?'

'Not really. I still have a bit of time. It's not much of a choice either'.

'You like Geography though, right?' says Mom.

'Not really'.

'I thought you couldn't stand the history guy, what's his name again?'

'Cage', says Michael, pointing.

'Yeah, but Geography is so boring. At least History is about actual people'.

'Written by the winners', says Michael.

Mom finishes her drink and pours another. 'Okay so History. What else, Drama?'

'Nah'.

'But you love performing'.

'Not really. I'll probably do French cos you have to do a language, and I was thinking of doing P.E'.

'You're brother chose those'.

'I know'.

'He got As'

'I know, Mom'.

'Tabitha is doing textiles?' says Michael.

I nod. 'That's one of the technology ones, like Design or I.T or Food'.

'Food?', says Mom, 'For a GCSE?'

'Food Tech. We've been doing it this term. It's nutrition and research and you get to build your own menu. It's pretty cool'.

Mom scoffs and drinks more.

Michael taps at an imaginary keyboard, 'Computers. Can't go wrong with them'.

I take another mouthful. Mom's nodding.

'Michael's right. Best to stick to the solid ones and avoid the Mickey Mouse subjects. You want a solid foundation for your A' Levels'.

'If I do A Levels'.

'Excuse me?'

'I'm just saying. There's different paths'.

'Such as?'

Michael chips in, 'I think Ferran's just considering all the options. Right?'

'Yeah'. I say.

'I see', she presses the side of her head, 'and have you spoken to your Dad about it?'

'A little bit'

'And what does he think?'

'I dunno. He said to go with my gut'.

'I bet he did. Another thorough Theo Burke analysis'.

She stabs at her food. I eat slowly.

'I'll get more garlic bread', says Michael, taking the plate and heading out
of the room.

Diabetes (– means somebody not speaking because they're about to blow a fuse)

There's no sugar
Try the cupboard
I tried the cupboard, Emile, there's none there
Okay
I need sugar. Tea without sugar's like drinking bath water
That's disgusting
I know! Where's the sugar?
Maybe it's gone
What are you drinking?
A drink
Is it tea?
It is
Does it have sugar in?
Course. Tea without sugar is grim.
So you finished the sugar?
I suppose I did
Why didn't you just say that?
You didn't ask
Do you enjoy being a dick?
I'm not sure
What am I supposed to drink now?
Anything you like
I like tea. A cup of tea starts the day
So have one

–

Look, I'll be gone soon and you'll have all the sugar and tea to
yourself

—

You shouldn't over do your sugar intake anyway, remember that
study I told you about?
You're drinking sugar right now!
Yeah. Delicious
I hope you get diabetes
That's not how it works, Ferran
I don't care. I hope you drink that tea and get diabetes and your
feet fall off
That's a bit harsh
Yeah, well, you shouldn't ruin someone's morning tea.

Options.

What you choose now will decide the shape of your future

What you choose now **could determine the rest of your life**

What **you choose** now

from a handful of options
you would never choose if you had any
real actual choice
at all
will
set **you on a course**
for either happiness or tragedy
so take your time

think this through

but hurry up

this is **big**

huge really

we're talking about the shape of your   FUTURE
the colour of your life
make sure you choose right
*What subjects do you enjoy? What do you want to do? Who do you want
to be?*

What career do you see yourself pursuing?

Make sure your choices are
your own
think it through
take your time

Hurry up

completed forms must be on

Miss Tallow's desk before

half term.

Come As You Are.

Kurt Cobain died.
People were crying at school and Ms Martin made an
announcement
in assembly that she was available to talk if anyone needed to.
Emile has been blasting the MTV unplugged album since he got
home.
Dad's got his first session booked in at the studio so dinner is on
me.
I check the cupboard and see baked beans, spaghetti and tinned
tomatoes.
There's cheese in the fridge and half a loaf of hard dough in the
bread bin.
I spot half a garlic bulb in the fruit bowl and an idea sparks.
I go to the living room, load up *Gap Band IV* and turn the speakers
towards the kitchen, then roll up my sleeves and get to work.

Ferran's Toast Pizza.

1. Choose the right music. Something Funky e.g. Curtis Mayfield

2. Fire up the grill cos it takes AGES to get hot

3. Toast the bread half as long as usual. I use setting number 1

4. Put little bit of oil in small saucepan and add chopped garlic
   ↑ 2 clov

5. Pour in tin of tomatoes, good pinch of salt and pepper and give good stir

6. While you wait for that to bubble, grate some cheese and click on the kettle
   ↑ Big handful

7. Put the part-toasted bread on a tray and spoon over two spoonfuls of garlic tomatoes on each slice, make sure to get right to the edges!

8. Cover with grated cheese

9. Add few drops of hot pepper sauce (Encona is the best)

10. Grill until cheese melts and goes golden and gorgeous

11. Let it cool down while you make your tea

12. Get comfy and eat like a boss!

Mickey Mouse.

'Is that weed?'

'Relax. Open the window will you?'

I do what I'm told, then sit on his floor with my plate.

Emile lights the spliff, takes a long drag and coughs.

He sets up one of his hippy sticks and lights it, coughing again.

The incense is to cover the smell.

'So you can handle Cage if you get him?'

'I hate him'.

'So why choose it?'

'Cos fuck him. He doesn't own History'.

'Ha ha! Gwaan little bro, stick it to him!'

He takes another long pull and sees me staring.

'It's just a bit of hash. Nothing major. Helps my head'.

He stubs it out and wafts the smoke towards the window.

'People say some subjects are Mickey Mouse'.

'Who said that?' He takes a bite of his toast. 'Yo. This is dope!'

'I dunno. People'

'People say a lot of shit, Ferran', he twists melted cheese over his bread.

'The whole thing is Mickey Mouse, man. It's all just a game. This is level one. You have to play it your own way'.

And right then, it hits me that he's leaving. He won't be here any more.

'You okay?'

'Will you still come home sometimes?'

He moves to the edge of his bed, 'Course I will'.

I nod. He kicks my foot, 'Especially if you keep cooking'.

He smiles and I want to ask if I can just sit here, while he works, curl up on the carpet and rest.

'You're gonna be fine, Ferran. You're tough. Just go with your gut'.

I smile back. 'That's what Dad said'.

Emile nods.

'He's not as dumb as he looks'.

Different Shapes.

'What the matter, darling?'
Nan scoops up her pile of yam skins and smiles
I look down and realise I've been peeling the same one
over and over.
'I have to make choices', I say, 'about the future'.
'Future is it?' she drops the skins into the bin, 'I see'.
'It's all so confusing. And everyone else seems so sure'.
She starts dicing the yams with the cleaver.
'Is what your belly say?'
I hold my stomach. 'I don't hear it saying anything'.
'Oh dear'.
Sophia is the only other person in the cafe, over by the window.
'I should be more like Emile', I pass Nan my peeled yam, 'He
always knows what he wants'.
Nan puts down her knife.
'Remember when you two used to help me with the dumplin?'
'Yeah'.
'Is what you remember?'
'I remember Emile doing all the different shapes'.
'And you?'
'I just did simple round ones'
'And why you do it so?'
'Because you said when we do it too fancy fancy they come out
tough'.
Nan smiles.
'And who's dumplin you remember eating?'

Yard.

I've been to Jamaica once. I was only like six, but it's still vivid.
The heat hitting my face, running up my nose we walked from the
plane to the baggage claim.
Watching the road whizz by through the hole in the floor of Uncle
Lester's car.
Pops' family live in the mountains and driving up
the narrow winding roads was amazing.
Mom was terrified the whole way, holding me tight with one hand,
gripping the door with the other.
We drove over to where Nan's family live and saw the foundations
of the house Nan and Pop's were building for when they retired.
There was a goat living on the patch where the bathroom was
going to be. It didn't have a name.
We stayed in a hotel in Montego Bay because of the mosquitos
at the country house.
Uncle Lester said Mom must have sweet blood and licked his gold
tooth.
I remember the yellow trampoline in the sea and Mom and Dad
drinking red drinks
through straws.

When we drove to the country, Emile disappeared all day with cousins.

One day he got bitten by ants and came back crying more than I'd ever seen him cry.

I remember someone's dog had puppies and I was going to name one, but they all died

before we left because somebody put rat poison down through the fence.

Mom was always surrounded by people, everybody wanted to talk to her,

especially the men.

I remember watching a tiny lizard running across the taps

as I brushed my teeth and Dad being quiet most of the time.

We had frozen grape juice every day and Uncle Lester showed us how to slice

open a coconut, drink the milk and scoop out the jelly.

The last night, we ate soup from a pot big enough for me to fit in and

I couldn't see the goat anywhere.

Lady Day.

Music and food in the air.

The cafe is busier than I've seen it in ages.

There must be nearly a hundred people here to celebrate Nan and say goodbye.

She's supposed to be taking the night off, but she can't help shouting orders and overseeing.

I'm collecting plates and glasses while Patrick and Sophia handle the food.

Aunty Marsha is up with cousin Leon who we haven't seen for years and now looks like Apollo Creed.

The four men on stage are old friends of Pops.

They look like an album cover in their perfect suits.

It's bebop and old time jazz. Later on there's a singer and then Dad is DJing.

I've already had three different women call me Emile and then feign shock

when I explain that I'm Ferran.

'It never you!'

'But, wait. See lickle one turn big fish now!'

'Lord have mercy!'

All the smaller kids are dressed up in their church clothes, scurrying around with their fried chicken.

Dad is near the back door with a red stripe keeping a low profile.

He dodged Patrick's requests for him to get on the drums, pretending to arrange records for later.

Dexter and Lenny are drinking rum cream nodding to the musicians every time
a new tune starts.
About an hour in, Dad gives me a camera and tells me to take pictures.
It's one of Mom's old ones.
'Maybe Emile should do it', I say, 'I don't want to mess up'.
'You'll be fine. Just point it and click'.
He gives me more film and waves me off.
I take some warm up ones of the kids climbing on cousin Leon and the guys on stage.

When the woman turns up in her long trench coat and movie star makeup,
all the men straighten their ties and pat down their hair.
The tall man with her looks like he walked off the set of a black and white gangster movie.
His guitar case could just as easily be holding a tommy gun and grenades.
I snap it all.
Patrick and Dad have been drinking brandy together since the food finished and as they help
set up the stage, they giggle like naughty school boys.
Nan makes a speech, thanking everyone for coming and for years of support.
Patrick will be running the cafe from now on, with Dad's help.
When she starts crying, Sophia goes up on stage and hugs her.

Everyone cheers and gives a round of applause. I reload just in time
to catch it and,
when Patrick blasts Nina Simone's 'My Baby Just Cares for Me',
Nan doesn't tell him
to turn it down.

I'm outside for some fresh air.
Patrick let me have a little rum cream and my face feels hot.
The dark street is peppered with lit up windows.
I sit down on one of the metal chairs and think about Lana. Where
is she? Is she with Taylor?
Are they kissing under a lamppost right now?

   I hear a giggle and spot two figures across the road in the
   shadows by the bottle bank.
It's Emile and a woman in a black dress.
He has his back to me, she is pressed against the wall.
They're kissing and whispering to each other.
I feel weird watching, but I can't look away.
Her arms are wrapped around him, one leg lifted around his thigh.
The cafe door opens and Patrick sticks his head out. Emile and the
woman freeze.
I turn away like I wasn't watching. I can hear a bass and drums
warming up inside.

'They're about to start. You should capture this' says Patrick.
'The singer?'
Patrick's smile widens. 'Your old man'.
As I follow him back inside, Emile steps out of the shadows.

I can't remember the last time I saw Dad
sitting down at a kit.
I can see from his eyes that he's at least half drunk,
Patrick must have finally broken him down.
He's very underdressed, but he looks happy.
>The fifty of so people still here are all turned in their chairs
to watch
and with the corner lamps and the dark outside, it feels like
we're at a proper gig
in some old jazz club.
>>The singer woman's sequin dress is as red as her
lipstick and she fills
all of it. Her gangster bassist is talking to Dad as she
introduces
herself.

Then they start playing.
Dad brushing the snares like he's hanging with old friends
and the woman's throaty voice is thick and amazing.

I take pictures;
>The three of them from the side and a few
>focused in on Dad.
>A woman with braids smiling and raising her
>glass.
>A little girl in a white dress and bunches passed
>out on her big sister's lap.
>Nan swaying with closed eyes.
>Patrick offering his hand.
>The pair of them slow dancing in the corner.

>Emile comes in as they start the second song.
>Dad gives him a nod.
>Emile nods back and comes to stand next to
>me at the counter. He smells

like perfume. He looks at me and points at Dad.
>I just shrug, then point the camera at his face and

>click.

YEAR 10.

where you're looking for one thing and
you find something else.

<u>Playlist.</u>

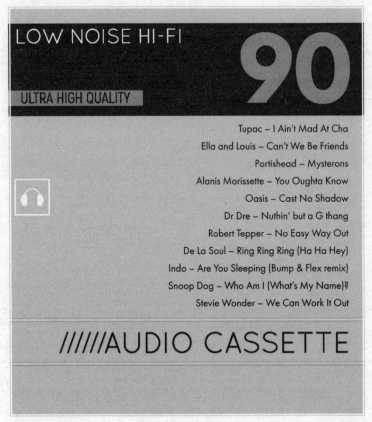

LOW NOISE HI-FI

90

ULTRA HIGH QUALITY

Tupac – I Ain't Mad At Cha
Ella and Louis – Can't We Be Friends
Portishead – Mysterons
Alanis Morissette – You Oughta Know
Oasis – Cast No Shadow
Dr Dre – Nuthin' but a G thang
Robert Tepper – No Easy Way Out
De La Soul – Ring Ring Ring (Ha Ha Hey)
Indo – Are You Sleeping (Bump & Flex remix)
Snoop Dog – Who Am I (What's My Name)?
Stevie Wonder – We Can Work It Out

//////AUDIO CASSETTE

	Y	N
Do you enjoy animals?		
Do you prefer being inside or outdoors?		
Can you work well with others?		
Do you enjoy crosswords or puzzles?		
Are you a person who likes to plan and/or strategise?		
Is job satisfaction dependent on salary?		
Are you interested in providing a public service?		
Have you ever operated a tractor?		

Farm Life.

'So, Food Tech?' she sips her coffee, staring at her new computer screen.

Behind her on the windowsill, the spider plant has had babies.

'I get it. Carving your own path'

'I just like food, Miss'.

'Right'.

She taps at her keyboard. 'I see you went with P.E., like your brother'.

'I guess'.

'How is he by the way, get the results he needed?'

'Four As. He's in London now. Goldsmiths'.

'Wow. Good for him. I knew he'd go far'.

I picture Emile and Dad loading up the car. Emile giving me a hug, then a dead arm.

Standing in the doorway of his empty room.

'Did you complete the careers quiz?'

'Yes, Miss'.

'And?'

'It said I should be a farmer'.

'Right. I see.'

'I've never even been to a farm'

'No'.

And we both laugh.

'It's a new software. It'll develop as they add more careers. It's nice to see you fighting gender stereotypes anyway. Men in the kitchen. Good for you'.

I picture Lana.

Overhearing her saying she was choosing Food Tech had absolutely nothing to do with me choosing it. Not at all.

'I have to say though, your end of year exams were quite disappointing'.

I look down.

'And it says here you were getting detentions regularly in the summer term?'

'Just silly stuff, miss. Nothing major'.

When I look up she's smiling.

'It can happen, that year nine slump'.

I nod.

'You know I'm a little sister?'

'Miss?'

'My older sister, Claire, she's quite a force. Growing up, it was tricky sometimes, finding my own space'.

I don't want this. I know she means well, but

'Can I go, Miss?'

'Excuse me?'

'Sorry, it's just, I wanted to get a tea before break finishes'.

Awkward silence.

'Yes. Okay. That's fine. I think we're done'.

I reach the door.

'Ferran?'.

'Yes, Miss?'

She smiles. 'You can do whatever you want to do. Remember that'.

I turn the handle and corridor sounds flush in.

'Yes, Miss'.

I have

all kinds of thoughts
about her
thoughts like
waking up in the middle of the night and she's there
in my room
by the window and the curtains are open and
it's a full moon so I can see that her
hair is up in a bun and
she's wearing the Chicago Bulls varsity jacket
that aunty Marsha got me and it's open and
she's got just knickers underneath
Hey
she says smiling and the air is thick and

I can feel myself breathing as she steps forward and
as she reaches the bottom of my bed I see
the edges of curves and
the smooth skin around her belly button down to the edge
of her knickers and
my blood is thumping as
she leans forward and
the jacket falls open and

those kind of thoughts

you know?

like   all the time.

That's okay right?   That's not wrong.

New Signing.

Cello's in goal.
He looks for me every time he gets the ball
in his hands.
The others aren't used to me playing and the fact that
I'm alright on the ball is confusing them.
I take advantage and score twice before
Jordan hacks me down.
'What? I got the ball', he says, grinning over me.
As I pick myself up, I look through the mesh fence.
Si and Pav are deep in conversation over
on the old bench.
I pick myself up
dust myself down and run
after the ball.

Cello's All Stars 94'

Seaman

Parucci   Adams   Baresi   Maldini

M. Laudrup   Desailly   Hagi

Baggio   Cantona   Giggs

First Lesson.

I sit on the back table with Michelle.

She looked surprised to see me, but smiled as I sat down.

She's had her hair cut into a bob with bits either side that flick up like mini ski ramps.

There's only fifteen people in the class and the only other boy is Bryan,

the chubby kid Taylor and them give grief to in P.E.

I nodded at him as I took out my pencil case, but he cut me a look like

I'd gate crashed his birthday party.

Lana is near the front, sitting with Susie and another girl who's name I don't know.

It feels a bit weird not having anyone with me, but also kind of cool.

Like I'm the new kid or something.

Miss Feeney is pretty chilled.

We all get A3 folders for our coursework, a tour of the kitchen and a long talk about hygiene. Meat always gets its own chopping board.

Each open plan cooking station has one of those cool magnetic strips that the knives stick to and there are actual proper cleavers like from *Big Trouble in Little China*.

I think about the old wood-handled machete that Pops used to keep by the back door for chopping sugar cane and bread fruit.

I keep quiet when Feeney asks if there are any questions.

Bryan wants to know if we can use the kitchen in break times for prep.

He seems pretty serious.

And he seems to know Lana really well somehow.

For homework we have to choose a dish that matters to us to talk about next time.

'Does a happy meal count?' I joke to Michelle as we pack up.

She looks at me like I just offered her an actual dog shit and leaves.

Bryan is laughing with Lana and Susie as they walk out like we're in his actual house or something.

I tell myself it's okay. It's just first lesson.

I'll get my chance.

Empty Space.

I've been coming in here a lot.
Sometimes I lie down on his bed and imagine I'm him.
His turntable, speakers and all
the good records are gone.
The empty dresser looks sad without them.
          I found one of his old journals.
It's one of those red and black ones with the thick cardboard cover.
I haven't opened it, even though
I want to.

Now it's just me and Dad I feel
like I'm supposed to do something.
To mark my territory.   Claim the space.
If we were wolves I'd be peeing in every corner and
rubbing my arse on the sofa or something.
I'm not a wolf

so I cook.

Viz.

We're sitting at the back.

Cage is talking about political propaganda and always questioning your sources.

I'm taking notes. Cello is pretending to. It's nearly lunch and I'm starving.

Cello knees me under the desk and nods at his book.

He's drawn a cartoon in the back of Cage with a massive head and snarling, drooly mouth.

He's got him wearing a t-shirt that says DICK across the chest. I laugh behind my hand.

'Is Joseph Goebbels funny to you, Mr Burke?'

Cello quickly flips his book to the front. I sit up. 'No, Sir. Not at all. Definitely not'.

'I should think not'.

Cello knees me again. I keep a straight face. Cage goes back to his lecture.

I take Cello's book and turn to the back. A quick check to see if Cage is watching, then I draw him the biggest, dangliest pair of balls you've ever seen.

Marcello Marco Angelo Antonio Tardelli.

Cello's Dad is Italian, his mom is English. They're both very
Catholic.
He has an older sister called Maria who's already left home
and a younger brother called Alex who's in year five.
He went to junior school with Taylor and Jordan.
He supports Man Utd and Inter Milan and shaves his top lip twice
a week.
He knows a lot about cars and formula one racing.
He's obsessed with Tupac and has watched *Juice* fifty times.
We compare rappers in Science and do Fantasy Football teams in
our books.

Sauerkraut.

I only remember the homework just
as I walk through the door.
Michelle is hugging her bag on her lap like a baby.
'What did you choose?' I say, hoping it will give me an idea.
'I'm not telling you', she says, like we're in year five or something.
Miss Feeney wants to know what dish people have chosen and why.
She says our relationship to food is like our relationship to
ourselves.
The stories behind things make them matter.
Everyone seems to talk about their mom and memories
of licking cake mix out of the bowl or rolling pastry and getting
covered in flour.
I picture Mom waving a tea towel through a cloud of black smoke
the one time she tried to make brownies.
Then I think of Nan and eating stewed chicken with Emile in the
cafe.
The rich dark sweetness of the meat and gravy on top of fluffy rice
and peas.
I could say that, but everyone else's food seems so English.
I don't want to be the odd one out.
Lana talks about making apple crumble with her Grandma.
Bryan gives like a ten minute monologue about roast chicken and
the importance of crispy skin which, I can't lie, actually makes me
kinda hungry.
I'm prepping myself to just say fish and chips and make something
up
about a trip to the seaside when Michelle says, 'Sauerkraut'.

She pulls a jar out of her bag.

It's full of something pale, shredded in a liquid.

A few people screw up their faces.

Michelle holds it up and smiles. 'It's shredded cabbage fermented in salt and water'.

There's a few groans around the room and somebody near the front says, 'Yuck'.

Miss Feeney shushes everyone. 'Brilliant! Is that homemade?'

Michelle nods. 'I made it last week'.

'It's a week old?' says Susie.

Feeney is beaming. 'Amazing! It's a super food. So good for your gut bacteria'.

More moans.

'Is there a story behind it for you, Michelle?'

Michelle puts the jar down. 'My mom used to make it'.

Murmurs go round the room. Michelle turns sheepish and puts the jar away.

'Thank you very much, Michelle. I'd love to taste some if I may. Who's next? Mr Burke?'

Everyone looks at me. Lana's face. I think of Nan and stewed chicken. Then I look at Michelle, shrinking into her bag.

'Fish n Chips, Miss'.

Number 5.

Short Circuit is on.

I haven't seen it since I was little.

Watching now, I'm realising how messed up it is that the guy playing the Indian scientist is the guy from the Mario Bros movie and not Indian at all. His accent is crazy.

Mom and Michael don't seem to notice from the sofa. Sadie is already in bed and they're more interested in nibbling each others ears than watching the film.

I just crunch my popcorn, swig my Dr Pepper and pretend not to see them.

I've got a stack of homework to do for Monday that I haven't even started yet.

Year ten is way more full on.

When the film finishes, it's eleven thirty. Michael makes a big show of yawning.

'That's a great movie', he says checking his watch, 'I'm bushed. I might hit the hay'.

Mom yawns too. 'Yeah. I should check on Sadie. You okay, love?'

'Yeah, I'm good', I say, 'I might watch some MTV'.

Michael takes their bowl and glasses to the kitchen. Mom comes over and rubs my head.

'Don't stay up too late, okay?'

'I won't'.

I listen to them giggling as they head upstairs, waiting until I hear their bedroom door close,

then I slide onto the sofa and switch to the

shopping channel.

Fade Away.

We're getting changed for basketball.

The GCSE P.E. group is pretty much the boys who are good at sports and Liam Dakin who genuinely seems to be here just to take the piss.

Mom and Michael got me the bred Jordan IVs for my last birthday and wearing them in school always feels brilliant. Cello's blue suede Patrick Ewing's are clearly fake.

I feel more confident in here lately. My body is definitely catching up.

I'm tying my laces when a pair of balled up socks smacks the wall in between me and Cello.

I know Jordan's laugh before I turn around. I'm about to have a go, when Cello picks them up.

Jordan laughs. 'Yes, Cell', he sets himself for a volley. Cello throws them up and Jordan boots them into the toilet cubicle.

'Goal!'

He fakes crowd applause then goes to fetch his socks. Cello looks at me and shrugs.

His relationship with them lot is so confusing.

On the court I'm average.

I don't panic, but I keep double dribbling and the urge to kick the ball every time it comes near is a constant fight.

I'm taller now though, so I can hold my own and get more of the ball

than I probably should.

I definitely wouldn't want to see my shooting stats.

Me and Cello are on Jordan's team against Taylor and the others.
Jordan and Taylor can both lay up easily and boss us around,
shouting where to go.
And I like it.
Being in the game. The focus and the tussling. The sweat and the
shouting and high fives.
I feel awake and like things makes sense.
'Who knew, Burke?'
Says Mr Evans at one point after I give a sweet pass
through to Jordan for a score,
'Maybe there's more of your brother in you than we thought'.

Shadow.

I am not Emile. **I am Ferran.** I am not Emile. **I am Ferran.**
Ferran Burke.

Demo.

'Afternoon, sir',
Patrick is rolling dough into a long sausage.
He wears an apron and a neckerchief now he's in charge,
but there's a sadness in his movements since Nan left.
The big silver pot is bubbling away behind him on the stove
the smell of all spice and onion.
Ella Fitzgerald is asking Louis Armstrong if they can be friends.
Sophia is playing patience with an old deck. Dexter and Lenny are
in their spots.
Patrick points at a thick envelope on the table. 'Finally got them
done'.
It's the photos I took back at Nan's leaving do.
'Man, I forgot all about these!'
There's a few blurry ones, but some of them are really good.
The ones of Dad look like they could go in an album sleeve or
something.
'You've definitely got an eye', says Patrick, 'I'm going to get a
couple up on the walls. If that's okay with the artist, I mean'. He
winks.
'Okay', I wink back.
Looking through all three packs again, the pictures of him and nan
together seem to be missing.
I get a flash of Emile and the woman kissing in the shadows and
Lana pops into my head.
She's in her P.E. kit, smiling, moving towards me.
'She must be special', Patrick says, snapping me out of it.
'What?'

He smiles to himself, 'That kind of sigh only comes for somebody
worth it'.
I shake my head. 'I'm just tired'.
'Of course. Yes. Forgive me'.
I put the photos back and watch him twist off little balls of dough,
rolling them into spinners for the soup. He lines them up on the
board like chess pieces.
'Who taught you to cook, Patrick?'
He finishes the last spinner before looking up. 'A very special
woman'.
His smile lets me know he means Nan.
'Did she know you liked her?' I say, feeling bold. There's an
awkward silence.
'Sorry', I say, 'None of my business'.
I take out my planner. It's covered in scribbles.
Patrick drops the spinners into the soup and gives it a stir.
'He was good to me, your Pops', he says, rinsing his hands in the
sink. 'When they let me out, he gave me a job and a bed'. He nods
to himself. 'A good man'.
There's a moment when I think he's going to say more, then the
door to the back opens and Dad walks in with a woman.

She doesn't look much older than Emile, maybe twenty, twenty
one,
she's dressed like she's going clubbing, her glossed lips sparkling.
We all watch as she fixes her jacket, sharing more skin than anyone
needs to.
Dad stands behind her looking sheepish.
'Ferran, what a surprise!'

'You're dropping me to Mom's, remember?'

'Course I do. Yeah. This is Chantelle. I'm helping her with some tracks. Chantelle, this is my boy, Ferran'.

Chantelle waves and tugs at her short skirt. I wave back.

'The super brainy one?' She says.

Dad puts his hand on her shoulder, 'Chantelle's a real talent. Great voice. Are you hungry? Pat, can we fix a plate please?'

Chantelle shakes her head. 'I'm alright, thank you. I need to pick up my son. It was nice to meet you all'.

'Hold on, don't forget this'. Dad hands her a CD. 'Listen through and see what you think about the strings. We can work on it again next week'.

He walks her to the door, her heels clicking on the tiles.

Sophia flicks Patrick a look of disapproval.

Dexter and Lenny go back to their game.

Walk Through.

Sometimes an empty house
feels amazing
like everything belongs
to you
and all the space is
yours
like a brand new
notebook
or an untouched snowy garden something
full
of potential and no
rules.

Other times an empty house
feels more like
an abandoned village
or a broken bike
chained
to a lampost

a graveyard of cool things
that happened, but
won't
any more.

Band Stand.

I made sure to be late.

It's one of those bright, but cold days.

They can all see me coming and I have to concentrate on not tripping over.

This might be a big mistake.

Lana and Kayla and a few other girls are huddled round a magazine. They all have the same stonewashed jeans. It's exciting being near her outside of school.

Taylor and Jordan are climbing over the railings and hanging upside down nearby. I know Lewis and Greg from school, but have never spoken to them. Cello is sitting on the edge of the bandstand biting his nails. He jumps down when I get close.

'Yes, Ferran'.

We bump fists. The girls look up. I raise my hand and smile. My heart is going.

'Not busy in the library, Burke?' Jordan lowers himself down and comes over.

He's wearing a lime green Cabrini ski jacket and baggy jeans. We're pretty much the same height now. I get myself ready for more jabs, then he says

'Is that real?' Pointing to my varsity jacket.

'Yeah. My aunt brought it back from America'.

He nods. 'Pretty sweet, ennit Tay?'

Taylor walks over. His black denim jacket makes his shoulders seem even broader. He has new Timbaland boots. I feel like I'm being auctioned or something.

'Nice', says Taylor, nodding.

And that's it.

The girls chat and giggle. The boys climb and dare each other to do stunts.

Every now and then one of them shouts something over about one of us and one of us shouts something back.

We argue about who would win in a fight between Bruce Lee and Mike Tyson.

Gregg turns his eyelids inside out and chases Amy. Taylor does a back flip.

After a couple of hours we walk round to the chippy on the high street.

Walking back to the park, drinking cans of Lilt, Cello gives me a nod that lets me know

I've passed the test.

Dummy.

The house is full of sound.

Long drawn out strings, thick gloopy sub bass lines, dusty drums and a ghostly female voice.

It's the kind of music that makes me think about the bottom of the ocean. Our house is the belly of blue whale. Dad is making coffee.

'What is this?' I say.

His smile is like a kid in a toy shop. 'Amazing isn't it? They're called Portishead'.

He spreads his arms and takes a deep breath like he's breathing in the sounds.

'I'm in love with it. Tea?'

'Yes please'.

I sit at the table, he sits on the sideboard and we just sip and listen.

The crackle. The scratches and reverb. It's all so warm. Sad, but in the right way.

Old and new   at the same time.

It's like somebody composed the perfect sounds for exactly where we are. I can't really

describe it.

It's like a dream.

Rain Check.

Emile called
to say he wouldn't be able
to come back for the weekend like he planned.
He has a lot of work and there's an event he has to arrange with a
society
or something and he didn't want to make us
fit plans around him.
Like we had anything
more important in our diaries.
Like the boxes on the calendar for this weekend weren't
completely full of block capital letters spelling
his name.

Fixed Values.

I don't understand.

Most things, if I concentrate, I can make them make sense, unpick them to the basic idea and then work forwards, but this, this just won't click. It's like hieroglyphics.

The seat next to me is empty.

I look across at Si and Pav, heads down already getting on with the questions.

I don't really speak to them these days, but I wish I was sitting closer to try and copy theirs.

'Just think logically', Miss Begum said, 'We're not computing, we're reasoning'.

I'm out of my depth. And I feel stupid.

These past months it feels like lessons are much harder.

'Are you okay, Ferran?'

'Yes, Miss. Fine. Just thinking'.

Just thinking *Get me out of here. What use is any of this in the real world anyways?*

Miss Begum goes to the door. 'I just need to pop to the office. Simon, you're in charge til I get back, okay? Everyone work through the questions, see where you get up to'.

As soon as the door closes, everyone starts chatting.

'Erm, we should probably just get on with the work', says Si waving his hands.

'Shut up, Simon', says Samantha with the curly hair.

There's a few laughs, then Michelle sits down next to me.

'What you doing?'

She takes my exercise book and starts writing in it.

'Oi'.

She shows me. She's done the first equation. 'It's not hard once it clicks, you just have to change your thinking a bit. I can help'.

'I'm fine', I say, pulling my book back.

'No you're not'.

'Get lost will ya'.

'Fish and Chips?'

'What?'

'All the food you could've chosen that matters and you chose fish and chips?'

'Shut up. Fish and chips matters to lots of people'

'I'm sure it does'

I look around. Nobody seems to be watching.

'What do you care?'

'I don't. I just didn't have you down as a chicken'.

'I'm not a chicken. What, just because I didn't pickle cabbage and bring it in?'

'Sauerkraut. I'll give you the recipe if you like'.

'Stick your recipe'

Michelle smiles. 'There you are'.

She gets up and points at my book

'I'll be in the library at lunch time if you want help with that'.

Journal.

It's empty
except for one page near the middle.
Like his thoughts are trying to hide from the outside.
There's no date so there's no way to know when he wrote it
I'm not sure if it's lyrics for a song or a poem or just words
I tried to hear his voice as I read it,
like when somebody reads a letter in a film, but each time
I read the words the only voice I heard
was mine

Ratio.

'So what's the deal with you and Michelle then?' says Taylor.

We're walking home in a pack. Him and Jordan lead, the rest of us following.

'What d'you mean?'

'I saw you with her the other day, by the library, laughing and that'.

'Me?' I can feel my defences raising.

'So, you two a thing?'

'What? Nah. Not at all'.

'Ferran likes a bit of weight on his women', says Jordan, stomping his feet.

The others laugh, except Cello.

'Piss off. She's just in my tech class'.

'She looks like a real goer', says Taylor, grinning, 'It's always the quiet ones that are the dirtiest'.

I feel my skin crawl and try to laugh it off.

Greg mimes stirring something in a bowl, 'Food Tech. The wettest subject alive'.

More laughing.

'Shut up, Greg. At least I can talk to a girl without shitting myself'.

'Ooh. Burn!' Jordan cackles and bumps shoulders with Greg. Greg gives me evils.

'I get it', says Taylor, walking backwards, 'Lana says it's just you, fat Bryan and loads of girls'.

The others look at each other. Greg's greasy face is calculating. 'That's like a 2:20 ratio'.

'Is it?' says Jordan.

'Pretty much', I say, 'Beats sweeping sawdust for Mr Nelson anyway'.

Cello is smiling. Greg spits. 'It's still wet. What do you even do?'

'Pretty much just eat stuff and hang with the girls. I'm not sure it's for you, Gregory. You'd probably pass out'.

Everyone laughs, except Greg.

Taylor is nodding, pointing at me like we're on the same page, 'Dark horse, you are Burke'.

And even though it feels icky

I smile like it doesn't

Wings.

I don't care about cars.
GTi and XR3i and TT and all the other letters don't get me going.
Nothing about horse power excites me.
A horse with powers, now that would be exciting. Like Bravestar's
horse with the shotgun
or that one from *Clash of the Titans* that can fly.
Cello and Taylor and the others all have cars on their walls.
Pictures of machines they one day want to buy and drive around.
They talk about driving lessons all the time, who's already driven
round Safeway's car park and who's gonna
get their license first when we're old enough.
Jordan's birthday is in September so it'll probably be him, but
getting into a car
with Jordan driving?
I'm good with the bus thanks.
The way they shout and get hyped when some flash car goes past is
the same way
they bark and whistle at girls outside the chippy and always makes
me wish

I could disappear.

Pegasus.

That's the name of the horse that can fly.

Like the Nike Airs Emile got in year seven when he won that chess tournament. Nike Air Pegasus.

I wanted a pair so badly.

I cut the picture of them out of the catalogue and stuck it on the side of my book case.

I'd look at it every night before I went to sleep and trace the swoosh with my finger.

I guess it's not so different to a car when you think about it.

Trainers that you could put on and fly away,

now that would be amazing.

Flown.

I read the number out and Dad dials.

It's Sunday morning and we're on the stairs.

The one letter Emile has sent home had less information
than a fortune cookie. And the number for his halls.

We rung every night this week and got nothing, so we're mixing it
up.

'We'll catch him in a hang over', says Dad, smiling, 'It's ringing'.

Tuna is rubbing herself against my legs.

'I should feed her'.

'Yes, you sh-hello? Is that Chesterman House? Yes, I'm trying to
reach Emile Burke, in room nineteen?'

His concentrating face is hilarious.

'Thank you very much', he cups the mouth piece, 'She's going to
get him'.

He fidgets with excitement.

'I'm just gonna feed her, Dad. I'll be right back'.

Tuna is attacking the food before I can even get it out of the tin.

'Alright, easy, greedy guts'.

I give her a tickle between the shoulder blades and leave her to it.

When I get back to the stairs, Dad is sitting with the phone in his
lap and a disappointed look on his face.

'That was quick'.

'He wasn't in. She said a bunch of them went out last night and we
should try Nicole's number because he crashes at hers a lot'.

'Who's Nicole?'

'I didn't ask'.

Chippy.

Now we can go off site for lunch　　　　we do.
Every day.
It's 80p for a regular bag, which is easily enough for two people even if you don't have a scallop.
We either sit on the wall outside, if there's no year elevens there, or we walk round
to the bus shelter by the library.
Taylor and Greg have got their hair cut like Liam Gallagher. Taylor can pull it off more than Greg.

　　　　Lana and the girls are all well into Joey Lawrence from *Blossom* right now, so they keep saying 'Woah' every two minutes in response to anything that happens.
It always ends up with a chip fight in the end. One time, Jordan stuffed the last of his saveloy in Lewis's pocket and even after he scooped it out, he stunk out the whole cloakroom.
Yesterday I saw Pav and Simon
walking past on the other side of the road.
For a second I felt to call out to them, but these lot would've definitely given them shit and
they probably would've pretended they didn't hear me anyway, so I didn't.
Taylor was throwing chips up and catching them in his mouth like a sea lion.
And just like the stupid press-ups, everyone, including Lana, seemed genuinely impressed.

Nuthin' But a 'G' Thang.

Dad's not home.

I take Cello to the kitchen and put the kettle on.

Tuna comes downstairs to say hi and be fed. I drop food into her bowl and make the teas.

'She's cute', says Cello as I hand him his mug.

'Yeah'.

I sit down across from him. He's the first person from school to come to our house.

'So your brother's at uni now?'

'Yeah. London'.

'Cool. I bet it's amazing'.

'I wouldn't know. He's pretty shit at keeping in touch'.

'My sister said he was kind of a big deal'

'She knew him?'

'Yeah. She said he was like some kind of genius or something'

'So they say'.

Cello blows his tea and sips. 'That sounds well annoying'.

'You have no idea'.

He lifts his mug. 'To the not geniuses'

'To the not geniuses'

We clink.

'Why do you hang around with them lot, Cell? All they do is give you shit'.

Cello squirms a bit. 'It's not so bad. Beats being a loner'.

He takes a sip. 'Plus, it's better now you're around'.

His smile is awkward.

'So it's just you and your Dad?' he says, changing the subject.

I nod.

'And the cat'.

Tuna looks over right on cue.

'That must be amazing', he says, 'Eat what you want, blast music and nobody gives you grief?'

I sip my tea.

'I guess. You hungry? I could make a sandwich?'

'I'm starving', he says, reaching into his bag and pulling out Dr. Dre's 'The Chronic' on tape.

'You got a stereo?'

I chuckle as I stand up.

'I think we might have. Pass it here'.

Flat Bread. (– means somebody not speaking on purpose)

Well I'd rather be weird than boring
Who's boring?
–

I'm not boring. Pass the flour.
–

How am I boring, Michelle?
–

What, cos I play football and don't watch *Star Trek*?
It's all relative I guess
And I'm relatively boring?
–

You're boring, how about that?
No. I'm weird remember? Don't over knead it. It'll get heavy
I'm not over kneading
–

I'm weird too you know
–

I am!
Okay
You don't know. How big do I roll them?
Golf ball size
How big's a golf ball?
Like this
This?
Bit bigger. Yeah, that's good.
–

—

I'm weirder than you.

Right. Hold the plate a sec

Trust me. I'm weird. I might not broadcast it all over the place, but I'm weird.

Yeah?

Yeah. I'm well weird.

Like how?

I dunno. Like ways. Weird ways. I do stuff

Okay. What do you do?

I dunno, I'm here for one. That's pretty weird, no? Ferran Burke, taking Food Tech?

Referring to yourself in the third person is weird

Shut up, man. Clean your surface.

Yes, chef

—

—

It is weird. Ask anyone. I shouldn't be here. Me being here is weird.

Why are you here then?

I don't know

—

—

Maybe you are weird after all

Loose Cannon.

His name is Clifford Packer and he's in year eleven.

He's loud and big and pushes people around and laughs like a donkey.

He's usually by himself because everyone with any sense stays out of his way, but sometimes he singles people out and goes at them in front of everyone. One time last year he smacked a kid with a dinner tray. Nobody grassed him up and he's done more since. This time is was me.

I don't know what I did or if it was just random bad luck. Me, Cello and Jordan were walking towards the lunch hall. Clifford was coming the other way, so we swerved to give him room, but he purposely side stepped and barged right into me.

I went flying into the wall and hit the floor.

'Watch where you're going bitch' he said. Cello and Jordan didn't know what to do.

As I got up I could see Lana and Kayla watching from the queue. Clifford did his donkey laugh with his big sloppy mouth. And then I just said it.

'Fuck you, Jabba'.

Everything seemed to stop. People who'd been walking by froze. The sounds from the kitchens seemed to mute.

Clifford was almost puzzled.

'What d'you call me?'

I knew I was in for it, but I could feel the lava in my belly and maybe it was Lana watching or maybe just the fact that his smug face seemed so sure that nothing would happen, but right there and then I didn't even care. A quick glance over at Lana.

'I said, Fuck you, Jabba The Hut'.

Then three things happened pretty much at the same time.

1. Mr Cage, came round the corner behind Clifford
2. Clifford growled and went to hit me and
3. I jumped on him first.

I'm so bored. Everything is
obvious. Copied and
predictable. Boys perv and bark. Girls
giggle and
destroy. Parents try and fail. Teachers
can't
see everything. People lock doors.
Poor People peer
through windows. Power saves itself.
Kindness seems naive.
Money drives everything. Egos
pen stories. Songs get written.
Photographs taken. Buildings
built. Families recycle. Roles
get replayed. Everything
happens. Nothing truly
matters. And the bored carries
on.

Boy Wonder.

'What the hell, Ferran? Where did this even come from?'
Mom is pacing like an army general with Sadie in her arms. Sadie keeps
giggling every time she turns and sees me. She calls everyone Baba.
'I don't know'.
We're in the kitchen at their house. I told Denise on reception to
phone Dad when they asked, but Mom must've given them her
new number after she moved, so she got the call.
I'm suspended for three days for violent behaviour. Clifford got a
week for repeat offending.
'That's it? That's all you have to say? I don't know?'
'I'm sorry'.
'Sorry? What if they'd wanted to expel you?'
'For one fight?'
'Ferran'.
She starts doing her calm down breathing. Sadie is really saving me
from a full attack here.
'I knew from your report last year that you were struggling, but I
didn't expect this'.
'Struggling? Who's struggling?'
The lava again.
'Ferran'
'What? Just because I don't get top marks in everything like,
Emile?'
'Leave your brother out of this'
'What, like you do?'
Maternal thunder stare.
'He started it, Mom. He pushed me. Ask anyone. He had it coming'.

'What does that even mean? You're in school, not prison!'
She holds her head. Sadie starts crying. Mom strokes her and gives her a kiss.
'I know. I know. I'm sorry sweet pea. Mommy got a little bit cross. It's okay. It's over now'.
She looks at me. 'I think you should go to your room and have a good think'.
'Whatever'.
'Excuse me?'
'Nothing'.
'Young man', she covers Sadie's ears, 'I don't care how big and bad you might think you are, I will slap that mouth off your face. Do you understand me?'
I feel like I'm five.
'Yes, Mom'.
'You're damn right, yes Mom'.
She takes a second to compose herself, then comes round the counter.
Sadie reaches out for me. Mom takes my hand.
'Sweetheart, I know there's been a lot of changes. It's a confusing and messy time, but we can't be silly. Acting up like this you're only going to hurt yourself, your future'.
And part of me wants to cry.
Part of me wants to say something horrible.
Part of me wants to run out.
All of me wants a hug.
But we can't hug.
Cos there's a baby in the way.

Ingvar Kamprad

Yo, did you smash?
Would you bang it?
I'd tap that
I would beat that up
You know I'm gonna hit that, right?

Why do boys talk about the most intimate acts as though
they're demolishing IKEA furniture?

Scotch Bonnet.

They look like little mini lanterns.

Some red, some yellow, some orange, all waxy and smooth.

'Don't touch your eyes', says Patrick, 'Even the outside can be hot'.

I'm behind the counter with him. Dad has a session day with Chantelle and is out back in the studio. He made me come with him so he could 'keep an eye on me'. He didn't give me a lecture like Mom, but his silence was just as loud.

The cafe is empty except for us. Dexter, Lenny and Sophia have gone to a funeral of someone they all knew. Patrick let me choose the music so I'm introducing him to Portishead.

I would be in English now, stealing glances at Lana. Instead I'm helping him prep jerk marinade, mixing spices while he washes chicken thighs over the sink.

I hold a shiny pepper up and twist it by the stem

'Have you ever eaten one, just like, raw?'

Patrick chuckles.

'I might have done. Trust me, I won't be doing it again'.

He starts patting down the meat with kitchen roll.

'Does it hurt?' I say.

Patrick touches his chin like he's thinking. 'I'm going to say yes. You want me to chop them?'

'No. I can do it'.

The door chimes and a man in a grey suit walks in holding a briefcase. Patrick sees him and immediately starts washing his hands. 'Mr. Saunders. I'll be right with you. Can I get you a drink?'

The man looks around like he's checking the place for mould.

'A coffee would be nice, thank you'.

219

Patrick pulls off his apron. 'Yes. Coming right up, take a seat, please'.

They sit at Sophia's table near the window and talk too low to hear over the music.
The man takes papers out of his briefcase and Patrick reads them.
I mix onion powder, thyme, all spice, black pepper, brown sugar, garlic, salt and ginger and rub it over the meat, then get a separate plate and start to cut the scotch bonnets.
There's a little yellow one that's daring me to eat it.
Patrick is shaking his head as the man speaks. He looks like he's being told off.
I drop the chopped peppers into the bowl with the spiced meat and massage it around, then wash my hands with fairy liquid and salt.
The ghostly voice is singing *Only You*.
The little yellow pepper is still there. Staring at me.

The man stands up and shakes Patrick's hand, then leaves.
Patrick sits staring at the papers for a while.
'You okay?' I say, as he walks back over. He looks to the back door, 'What time did your dad say they were taking a break?'
'Bout eleven, I think. Is something wrong?'
Patrick folds the papers up and starts putting his apron back on.
'I do hate banks', he says, inspecting the meat, 'This looks good'.
'Thanks'.
'Did you wash your hands properly?'
'Yep'.
He looks around. 'I'm just gonna. I need a quick cigarette'.
He goes out through the side door with a sigh.

I look at the yellow pepper. It's only as big as a fifty pence piece. How hot can it be?

I pick it up and sniff it. There's only a faint scent.

'I can handle you'.

I bite it off right down to the stalk and chew.

It's cold and crunchy and there's an immediate heat, but it's not so bad. I do a little skank.

'Ha ha! Who's a bad man?'

Then my whole head explodes.

Wet ; weak, timid, lacking in courage, strength or value
e.g.
It's just a head lock. Why you being so *wet* for?
or
Man, general studies is just *wet*.

Tough ; good, possessing positive qualities, tasty, attractive
e.g.
How *tough* is Kayla looking right now?
or
Yo, those trainers are *tough*!

Business.

Dad turns off the engine.

Fine rain sprinkles the windshield. The box of jerk chicken is warm in my lap.

My throat and ears are still tingling from the pepper.

'Is it bad?' I say.

Dad sighs.

'Yeah. It's pretty bad'.

'What will they do?'

'I don't know. We have to see if they agree to this loan, then we can re-assess the lease'.

'But we won't lose it, right?'

He taps the steering wheel like a metronome.

'But what about Patrick? And the others?'

'I don't know, Ferran'.

'There must be something we can do?'

'Well', he says, taking out his keys, 'I'm open to suggestions'.

Rep. (– means somebody not speaking on purpose)

Yo, it's me. It's Cello.
Easy, what's up?
Nothing. You good?
I'm fine
You get in trouble?
Not really. A bit.
Man your parents are so chilled. My Dad would've gone nuts
–
Everybody is talking about you
Like who?
Like everyone. You're like a legend or something
Shut up
I'm serious! You beat up Clifford Packer!
I didn't beat him up
Doesn't matter. You almost punched Cage too, it was so mad!
Pretty dumb
Jordan won't shut up about it. The girls too
The girls? What did they say?
Ah, now you're interested
Cello, what did they say?
I don't remember
Shut up! Tell me
They said that you're full of surprises
Who did, Lana?
Kayla.
Oh
You know she likes you right?

Shut up

I'm not joking

I'm not Jordan, Cello

Exactly. Everyone's going park tomorrow, you should come

I can't really. My mom.

I get it. So you back Monday?

Yeah

Want me to knock for you, walk in together?

Cool

I'll handle your press

Shut up

See you later, Rocky

Yeah. In a bit.

Food Group Table with Nutrients and Functions

FOOD GROUP	CONTAINS (nutrients	Functions	Examples	
1. Bread and cereals (grains)	• Carbohydrates (carbs) • Fibre	• Give us energy • Good for our digestion	• Pasta, rice, cereals, bread, potatoes . . .	
2. Fruit and vegetables (veggies)	• Vitamins • Minerals • Fibre	• Keep us healthy • Protect us from illness Good for our digestion	• Fruit: Bannanas, apples strawberries, • Veggies: Carrots, lettuce, cucumbers . . .	
3. Meat. fish and beans	• Proteins • Iron	• Repairs our body • Build muscle and make us strong • For growth	• Meat: Lamb, pork chops . . . • Fish: cod, sardines, tuna . . .	
4. Milk and dairy	• Calcium	• Keeps our bones and teeth healthy	• Milk, cheese, yoghurt . . .	
5. Good vegetable oils and fats	• Good fats	• Give us energy	• Olive oil, avocados . . .	

New Light.

Most people don't know anything about the fight, but the ones who do
definitely stare.

At break time I can feel eyes on me as we sit by the piano with our teas.

Jordan is re-enacting what happened, using Greg as his dummy.

I'm eating my biscuit, trying to play it cool, secretly loving it.

Kayla is next to me with Lana on the other side of her with Taylor.

'Have you seen him?' says Kayla, 'Clifford?'

'Yeah. He acted like he didn't know who I was'.

'Cos he's shook!' says Cello.

Kayla shuffles up closer so our thighs are touching. 'It was so cool'.

Jordan sees us close together and stops wrestling Greg.

I move towards Cello, making space.

Over by the hatches I can see Pav and Si, sitting with the other top setters.

Jordan tucks his shirt back in, 'Remember when I smacked that Kieran kid in year eight, Tay?'

Taylor shakes his head.

'I remember', says Greg.

'Shut up, Greg'.

'Wasn't Kieran in year seven?' says Cello.

Jordan gives him evils. Lana and Taylor laugh.

'Big man, beating up a little kid', says Kayla, smiling at me and slowly biting
her biscuit.
I smile back and wonder whether this is what Emile feels like
every day.

Obi Wan.

'How do you know all this stuff?'

Michelle doesn't look up.

'It's just science. On one level, the body is just a machine and food is the fuel, right?'

'I guess'.

'Right, so knowing what's in the fuel is pretty important. Nobody wants to fuel a machine on crap do they?'

'But what about taste?'

She looks up.

'Well, that's the art'.

I nod, staring over at Lana's table. She's explaining something to Bryan.

'Still going with the Jedi tactics, eh?'

'What?'

'Woo her with mind tricks'.

'What are you talking about?'

My face has gone instantly hot. Michelle goes back to the worksheet.

'Nothing', she says, 'Forget I said it'.

'I will'.

I pretend to read the textbook. Michelle rubs something out then gestures like she's casting a spell. 'Taylor isn't the droid, you're looking for'.

'Shut up!'

People on the next table turn round. I pretend to read. I feel naked.

'You're not funny', I whisper.

'Okay. Please don't beat me up, scary Ferran'.

She fake shudders, smiling to herself.

I grab the worksheet. 'We're supposed to be doing this together'.

Michelle folds her arms.

'Okay. Be my guest'.

Her smile reminds me of Emile's every time he'd beat me in an argument by

somehow making me

beat myself.

Line.

We need a different word for dick.

My dick.

Something about it doesn't feel right. It's too aggressive. Too harsh.

When you think about it, it's pretty weird that we call someone a dick

when they're being an idiot. Like the penis is an idiot.

Penis. That feels weird too. Penis. It's too sciencey.

If you're talking to a doctor, fine. I seem to have a problem with my penis, Doctor.

Okay, let me take a look. Fine. But anywhere else, penis doesn't work.

Willy. Too babyish. If you're in the infants maybe, but try saying it now. My willy. Just weird.

Prick. Same as dick.

Cock. Too porno.

In America they sometimes say junk. His towel fell down and we all saw his junk. Like it's the stuff you throw away. It doesn't make any sense.

Knob. I hear that one a lot. Yeah, Jordan got the football right in his knob. Knob. It's just not

a nice word to say is it?

It's mad really.

Surely we can come up with a word for a part of the human body we pay so much attention to, that doesn't feel aggressive or stupid or just plain weird. What's wrong with us?

Line.

My line.

That's kind of what it is, I mean what it looks like, sort of.

Line.

It's not aggressive or weird or an actual food.

My line.

Have you seen his line?

I think it could work. Line. There you go.

Yeah, cos I'm gonna introduce a new noun for the male sex organ. I'm gonna start referring to it as my line and it's gonna catch on and spread internationally and before you know it people world wide will be calling it their line and feeling really good about it.

Man, I'm such a dick.

Kid n Play.

'Stand up, Ferran Burke!'

My hand grips the note. Cello looks down.

'Bring it here' says Cage

'Bring what, sir?'

'Young man, you will bring that piece of paper to the front right now or I promise you, you will regret it'.

Cello is about to stand up with me, but I stop him

'Yes, sir. Coming'

I hold it out to him as I get to his desk.

'I don't want it', he says, 'I think we should all hear what it says'.

I shake my head.

'No, no, Mr Burke, I think we all have a right to hear whatever comedic masterpiece is more important to you than the D-Day landings. What does everyone think?'.

I turn around, the rest of the class are leaning forward, baying for blood.

Cello is looking at me like a puppy from a pet shop window.

'I don't think so, sir'. I say, swallowing hard.

'You don't think so?' his voice lowers a tone, 'You don't think so?'

He's up and round his desk leaning over me. 'You will read it out right now!'

I unfold the paper and look at our scribbled writing. We've been passing it back and forth

all lesson.

'Now!'

Another quick glance at Cello, then I feel myself floating up out of my body as I start to read.

'How many pages in a book called prick?

Must be six hundred at least, it's real thick

If I had his face I would really be sick

And I bet it's ten years since he's seen his own-'

He snatches the paper out of my hand. A room full of shocked faces. Cello staring.

I tell myself it must be a dream and try to wake up,

then I'm grabbed by the collar and dragged out of the door.

Tony's Plaice.

'Shut up!'

'I swear down. In front of everyone'. Cello is giddy as he relays what happened. We're on the wall outside the chippy.

'Bollocks', says Greg, 'J, is he lying?'

Jordan shrugs.

'Ferran? Did you?'

I nod. Kayla snorts, 'Oh, my God! What did he do?'

'I've got detention for the rest of the week'.

'Fair play, Burke', says Taylor. Lana watches me as she eats a chip.

'Did he keep the note?' says Greg. Everyone looks at him.

'What? I mean for like a keep sake or whatever. No?'

Kayla throws a fat chip at him. Greg catches it and throws it back. Kayla squeals.

Then it's pretty much a salt and vinegar free for all.

Midnight Caller.

Bottles are in the fridge.

Nappies and wipes are ready.

Spare dummies next to the cot and I've got enough muslins to open a shop.

Sadie's walking now. Basically falling forward until she hits something, but it's pretty cool.

Her words are coming too. I spent the hour before she went down trying to get her to say my name.

'Berran'

'Ferran'

'Berran Boo Boo'

'Okay then'.

Mom said they'll be back by ten the latest and the phone number of the restaurant is on the pad by the door.

I checked on her nine times the first hour. I've gone down to four since then.

Being a baby is easy.

I wanted to watch a film, but got scared I'd get distracted and not hear her, so I'm in my room pretending to tidy up.

I found some of last year's exercise books under my bed. And my planner. My doodles look proper young. I can see my progression at forging Mom's signature through the weeks.

Then I see her number.

I copied it into January 3rd because I found out that was her birthday, but bottled out of calling and forgot it was there.

The urge to phone her swells up.

I go to Mom and Michael's room to check the time. It smells like

234

Mom's perfume and the whole far wall is a mirrored wardrobe.

There I am. Standing with my planner.

7:55. That's not too late to phone someone on a Saturday night, right?

And say what?

She's probably not even in.

They have a cordless phone on the bed side table. I could ring right now.

Something about being on the other side of town feels safer. More anonymous somehow.

I go back to Sadie's room and check her. She's sleeping peaceful.

Enough Jedi mind tricks, Ferran. Time to act.

I sit down on their bed. The expensive duvet is like a cloud.

I pick up the phone to practise in the mirror.

'Hi, yeah, is Lana there please?'

Hang up.

Pick up.

'Hello, sorry to call late, I just wondered if I could speak to Lana?'

Hang up.

Pick up.

'Yes, tell her it's Ferran. I'm a friend from school?'

Hang up.

Stare at my reflection. Do or do not.

There is no try.

The button sounds are a slow melody. 0 1 2 1 4 2 9 . .
It's ringing. My chest feels tight and the receiver is shaking in my
hand. Ring ring. Ring ring.
Stare at myself. Ring ring. Ring r–
hang up.
Nah.
Bad idea. *How did you even get my number? You what? Are you stalking
me?*
Man, that was close.
That could've been awful.
Then the phone rings.

Panic stations.
I want to just leave it, but Sadie is sleeping.
If I answer, she'll know it's me.

Unless..

Character Improv ~~Idiot~~ Genius.

(– means somebody not speaking because they're shit at accents)

–

Hello?

–

Hello? You just called us?
Halo
Who is this?

–

You just rang?
No, I don't thank I deed
I just did 14713

–

Hello?
I'm sarry. Wrung noomber. I'm Scooottish. Bye Bye

We Gotta Problem Here?

We're doing *Julius Caesar* in English.
Mr Kelsey says it's one of the first gangster films
Deception, ambition, megalomania, betrayal.
When he talks about the story and the Brutus guy with the politics and the stabbing
he gets so excited, I honestly wish it made sense, but
as we read it out loud, there's something about the words on the page
that just make my head hurt.
So I spend the whole lesson imagining I'm Tre from *Boyz n the Hood*
replaying the movie in my head
Emile is Ricky and when he's running in the alleyway and
the guy leans out of the car with the shotgun
I accidentally scream out loud.

'Are you okay, Ferran?'
'Yes, sir. Sorry. It's just. Brutus, man. How could he?'

'HE LOVES TO HEAR ME TELL HIM HOW MEN CAN BE
SNARED BY FLATTERERS, JUST LIKE UNICORNS CAN
BE CAPTURED IN TREES, ELEPHANTS IN HOLES, AND
LIONS WITH NETS'.
ACT II, SCENE I.

Red Light.

It's break time.
I'm drinking my tea. Lana is telling us all about some weirdo
Scottish guy
who phoned their house on Saturday night.
'That's so creepy', says Kayla, nudging me, 'Isn't it?'
'Yeah', I say, 'Horrible'.
Lana shudders, 'I know! He was heavy breathing and everything'.
'Pervert'.
'Weird thing was, he said he was Scottish, but it was a Birmingham
number'.
'I bet it's a sex thing', says Greg, 'Like role play. I saw it on *Eurotrash*'.
Jordan laughs, 'Yeah, he gets naked and rings people to wank off'.
Him and the boys laugh. Cello looks at me. I stay silent. Lana
whacks Jordan.
'It's not funny! My mom wants to change our number'.
'Yeah, J. Shut up man', says Taylor, playing the good boyfriend. He
puts his arm around Lana, and grins at Jordan behind her back.

'Everything you see, I owe to spaghetti'
 – *Sophia Loren*

Love Bug.

'You wanna see something?'

We're in Cello's living room. His mom does the shopping on a Wednesday so the house is empty.

'See what?'

He disappears upstairs. I sit down with my cherryade. Their sofa is bumpy green velvet like Nan's old one and the gas fire bars are charred at the sides. I can smell herbs, but I'm not sure which ones. He said not to bother taking my shoes off when we came in.

Cello comes back in with a video.

'What's that?'

He slides back to sit against the armchair and opens up the brown cabinet underneath. Their VCR is even older than ours. Cello carefully loads up the tape, grabs the remote control and slides back to sit with his back against the armchair to my right.

'We don't have time to watch anything' I feel the fizz on my teeth, 'Form's in half an hour'.

'Hold on'.

He jumps up and closes the curtains, then sits back down and presses play.

It's a man and a woman in a lift. They're both dressed like they work in an office.

The colour contrast is really high like those American soap operas and there's cheesy saxophone music playing.

'What's this?'

Cello crosses his legs, 'Just wait'.

The camera zooms in on a fly, buzzing around, then landing on the woman's neck.

She slaps at it and curses.

I look at Cello. He points at the screen.

The woman groans and looks at the man. The man smiles. The woman licks her lips and takes off her glasses. The saxophone changes key. I look at Cello again, he points at the screen again.

'Love bug', he says.

The woman unbuttons her blouse and pulls down her bra.

'Holy shit!'

The man is acting like this is completely normal and holds her breasts. The woman groans again.

I can feel myself tingling.

The man drops to his knees and lifts up the woman's skirt. They both moan. The saxophone plays.

'Jesus, Cell. Who's is this?'

'My sister's boyfriend gave it to me. Crazy right? Imagine that was your job?'

'What if your mom comes back?'

'Relax. She always has coffee with her friend'.

The man and woman have swapped places now. She's on her knees, unzipping his fly. My trousers tighten. I lean forward. My heart is thumping.

'Holy shit!'

I've never seen one that big before in my life. The camera zooms in.

'Is this for real?'

I turn to Cello and he's not even looking at the screen, he's just watching

me.

Writers Room.

I smell perfume as I close the front door.
There's an instrumental I don't recognise on the stereo,
light, stabby strings and dusty drums.
Chantelle is sitting at the kitchen table with an open notepad and
pen.
'Hi, son', says Dad, leaning in the open back doorway with a
cigarette,
'You remember Chantelle?'
I nod and wave, strange woman in the house alarm bells ringing
inside my head.
'We're just having a writing session. Needed a change of scenery'.
He's wearing a short sleeved open paisley shirt with a white vest
underneath like it's summer and not December. Chantelle drops her
pen on the table.
'It's not happening, Theo. I got nothing'.
Dad flicks his butt and comes inside.
'You're trying too hard. Over thinking it. Just listen'.

Chantelle closes her eyes and tunes in. Dad closes his and starts to sway.

'Let it come'.

I drop my bag and go to the fridge. The strings make me think of yo-yos.

'Up and down', I say, taking out the ginger beer.

'What?' says Dad, opening his eyes.

I fetch a glass. 'Up and down. Like a yo-yo. That's what it feels like'.

Chantelle's eyes widen.

'Up and down'. She grabs her pen. 'Up and down, you got me', she starts singing the words, building a melody. 'You got me, up and down, again. I like it!'

Dad copies her melody, humming it to himself. 'Okay. Maybe'.

Chantelle is buzzing, writing words in the air with her finger.

'How many times, can I fall?' she smiles at me with her shiny lips, 'You're good'.

Dad chuckles to himself and nods.

I take my drink and leave them to it, whistling as I go.

Kapa Sigma Loser.

We're in the woods.
When the girls aren't with us is when I feel the most out of place.
I nod way more than I talk and every nod feels like a lie.
Greg stole a bottle of cooking sherry from his Nan's kitchen.
Jordan took a bunch of those vodka miniatures from his mom's
cabinet. Taylor somehow managed to get some random guy to buy
four cans of Carling for him at the Outdoor and Lewis has a half
empty bottle of gin.
The only booze we had at home was a couple of red stripes in
the fridge and the overproof rum from duty free. I couldn't bring
myself to steal from Dad, so I'm empty handed.
'We didn't have anything', I say when it's my turn.
Groans.
'Goody goody', says Greg.
'Shut up. I just don't live with alcoholics'.
'What d'you just say?'
He's about to get up, when Cello pulls out a long thin glass bottle
of something bright yellow.
'What's that?' says Jordan. Cello grins.
'Limoncello'.
'Ha ha! Cello's Limoncello'.
'Woah. That looks tough!'
'Me and Ferran nicked it from my mom. Ennit, Ferran?'
'Yeah, yeah. Fully'.
'The Italian Stallion', says Taylor, taking the bottle. 'Is it strong?'
'Thirty percent', says Cello.
'Wicked'.

'We should've brought a boom box'.
'You wanna swap?'
'No way!'
'How do we drink it?'
'What do you mean? With your mouth!'
We all laugh. And drink. And drink.   And drink.

Taylor

It's bullshit / because / no just because / because / she doesn't
want to and/ I don't want to be like/ I'm not a prick but / it's
been ages and / we'd be careful / I just / my lips are numb /
are your lips numb? / why are my? / do you know what I mean
though? / how long do I have to wait? / it's like / you know? /
should I push? /

Cello

I'm serious / you're special / you know? / shut up / I'm talking
shit / I'm just / don't even / I remember / you remember? / I
remember / you / what you did / is that? / nobody ever / shit
man / I can't even / it's you / you know? / fair play / I wish we
could just / oh god / I'm so / wow / wow

Me

Can I just / let's lie down / doesn't matter / I'm breathing / don't
tell my mom / cos / the baby / and / fuck Michael / you know?
/ you know? / fuck him / not really cos / I'm not / he's alright /
I'm just / you're a good friend man / I can't / can I just / sshhh /
it's a secret / the phone / but / it's like Patrick / I'm not Patrick /
Hatrick / Patrick scored a hat trick / Ha ha / is that? / that's the
moon / yo / look at the moon! / fucking hell / the moon / I'm
the moon man / the moomin/ I can control / the moon / and
tides and / I just / ah man / she can't see me/ and I'm / I'm / I'm
gonna puke

247

Pancakes.

Emile has a moustache.

His hair is a bumpy mess, but on purpose, and he's wearing a battered brown leather jacket.

I could feel the cold outside air when I came in, so he must've just got back.

There's still a week before we break up for Christmas.

'Yes, Ferran!' He gives me an actual hug, squeezing hard. I can smell his jacket as I look at Dad over his shoulder. Dad just shrugs. The Specials are playing in the living room.

'Getting big, little brother'. And I do feel bigger now he's standing right here and there's something about him that feels odd. If I didn't know better I'd say he seemed nervous.

'Does your Mom know you're back?' says Dad.

'No. No. I didn't. It was a spur of the moment thing, thought I'd surprise you'. His smile is weak.

'Right'.

'I'll go see her tomorrow. I wanted to come home first. You know?'

'Yeah. It's good to see you, son. Isn't it, Ferran?'

I pull a face like I'm not sure. They both laugh.

'Shall we get a Chinese?' says Dad, rummaging in the drawer.

Emile sits down at the table, 'Sounds great'. He looks tired.

I think it's been two phone calls of less than five minutes all term. I click the kettle on and fetch mugs. Dad pulls out a takeaway menu and sits down too.

'Come on then. Fill us in on uni life'.

Emile runs his hands over his head and sighs. 'Yeah. What can I say? Is that my cactus?'

'Yep', I say, 'Still not dead. Gemma would be proud'.

'Fair play. Gemma. Jeez, where's she these days?'

He ponders it. Dad flashes me a concerned look.

'Do we want duck pancakes?'

'Always', I say, putting teas on the table.

'Emile?'

'What? Yeah. No. Pancakes. Perfect'.

Valentines.

Kitchen noise and bustle. I'm washing up.
Rubber gloves creep me out, but these new taps are stupid hot and I'm wishing
I'd taken them when Miss offered.
I'm sure there must be some special Jedi technique for washing sieves, but I don't know it.
I'm basically just pushing muck from one side to the other over and over again.
Lana is washing up at the next station across. Every time I look up, I feel like she's just looked away.
Michelle wipes down our side board. Our flapjacks are cooling on the rack.
Everyone else used honey, but she brought in dark molasses from home.
I already know they're gonna be tough, in the good way.
'How long are you gonna wash that thing for?' She drops her cloth behind the taps.
'I dunno, until somebody explains how the hell you ever get it clean?'
'Just hold it under the running water'.
She bumps me out of the way and takes the sieve, aiming the tap and shooting off the bits.
'How do you know this stuff?'
She puts the sieve on the draining board and bows.
'Wow', I say, 'You really are Yoda'.
'I always felt more in tune with Chewy'. She growls the best
Chewbacca growl I've ever heard from a human and we both laugh

as we clean up.

'I didn't know about your mom', I say, handing her a bowl, 'I'm sorry'.

'For what? You didn't kill her'.

My stomach drops and I turn back to get another plate.

'Sorry', she says, 'I didn't mean that'.

'No. I get it. People always follow the same script, just to say something, don't they? It's so lazy'.

Her head tilts. 'You're a layered one, Ferran Burke'.

I bow like she did and pass her the plate. Miss Feeney says something about homework.

'What was she like?'

Michelle goes to answer, then stops herself.

'I'm an idiot. It's none of my business'

'No', she says, 'It's okay'.

She dries the mixing bowl.

'You know how when somebody dies and everyone is like, they were so special, truly an amazing person and you're thinking to yourself, okay, I get it, we have to be respectful and say lovely things and everyone is special to somebody, but amazing? Like actually amazing? Really?'

I have to smile. 'Yeah, I do'.

Michelle closes the cupboard. 'Well, she actually was'.

Sometimes it feels like you get to know more about a person
in one meaningful sentence, than in a whole year of pointless chat.
The bell goes and I pull on my blazer.
'You wanna meet here after school, split the flapjacks up?' She says.
'Yeah, cool'.
'Okay. See ya'. She smiles and leaves.
I tuck in my chair and fish in my pocket for coins
and then I find
the card.

Roses are red
Violets are blue
You touching me
Me touching you
xxx K xxx

Post Man.

'What's wrong with you?'

'Nothing. Why?'

It's home time and I'm walking with Cello towards reception.

'Mate, you've been acting weird all afternoon'.

'No I haven't. I'm fine. Has Jordan said anything to you?'

'About what?'

'I dunno. Him and Kayla?'

'Like what?'

'Doesn't matter. Forget it'.

'We going park with them lot?'

'No. I can't'.

'Why not?'.

'Erm, I've gotta go to my mom's. I'm babysitting'.

'Right. Well, call me tomorrow if you wanna do something. Maria got me the Snoop Dogg album and it'll sound tough on your speakers'.

'Yeah. Okay. I've gotta go. I left something in the kitchens. I'll ring you tomorrow'.

Pirate Radio.

I wake up to pee, which hardly ever happens. Must've been my dream.

It was me and Lana on a beach, I was building us a massive sand castle house, but the waves were getting closer and Kayla was surfing one, right for us.

On the way back from the toilet I hear muffled voices downstairs.

Emile showed up out of the blue at dinner, walking in like a celebrity, trampling all over me trying to talk to Dad about my tricky valentines card situation.

His hair is a decent fro now, like he thinks he's Huey Newton or something.

They started sipping rum after we had ice cream and were still going when I went to bed.

It's late enough now for the air to feel thick and they're still down in the kitchen.

They must hear me moving about because they go quiet, waiting for me to get back into bed.

I walk normally to my room, then tip toe back to the top of the stairs, treading on the edges of the carpet and lie down with my chin on the top stair, tuning my ears in to hear.

I can't make out what they're saying and their voices are so similar now I can't even tell who's speaking. There's lots of silence too, between the words. They must be be pretty drunk.

After a while I feel myself dropping off and rather than have them find me

passed out on the stairs, I tip toe back

to my room.

Anatomy of a Bruise.

Small veins and capillaries (the tiniest blood vessels) under the skin sometimes break. Red blood cells leak out of these blood vessels and those that collect under your skin cause that bluish, purplish, or blackish mark.

Deep Cover.

I'm hiding behind an oak tree.

Anybody seeing me would think I was playing a game of hide and seek. But this is no game.

Kayla is waiting for me over by the bandstand.

I'm supposed to go down to her so we can kiss. Her and Lana and the others arranged it.

They're all down on the playground waiting for us to come back after we've done it.

I told her I was going to the shop and planned to run home. Then I froze.

Now I'm stuck behind this tree.

If I leave, she'll see me.

If I come out, I'll have to go and kiss her.

It feels like there's not enough air.

I need something to happen. An earthquake or a thunder storm or an alien invasion.

What is wrong with me?

Most boys would love to kiss Kayla. She's year ten royalty and Jordan is well pissed off that she's into me. And she's nice. Scary, but nice. It's not her fault. It's me.

I'm the freak.

I want to, but I don't want to. I think about kissing all the time, so why can't I move?

I don't want to do it wrong. I want to be good at it. I want it to be brilliant. I want it to matter.

I want it to be Lana.

My first kiss is supposed to be Lana.

I'm supposed to take her face in my hands under a streetlight in the rain and kiss her like she's never been kissed before and the electricity of our lips together is supposed to make the streetlight surge and pop and when we open our eyes, we're both smiling and then 'Love Supreme' starts playing from hidden speakers.

Yeah, cos that's ever gonna happen.

I'm the last one.

Even Cello kissed Amy at New Years in the game of truth or dare, right before he threw up,

so it's just me. They don't know.

I told them all I kissed a girl called Gemma at Centreparcs last summer.

I told them she was older and really fit and that she wanted to have sex with me, but we didn't have any condoms so we just fooled around. I told them she gave me a cactus when I left.

None of that happened.

Mom and Michael went to CentreParcs with Sadie, I saw the photos, stole some details and made up a story just so they wouldn't call me frigid.

Kayla is the opposite of frigid.

I don't know how many boys she's kissed before, but it's definitely more than none.

And I'm supposed to be next.

My lungs are in my throat. My legs are jelly. Why am I not more like Emile?

The News

FREAK STORM ROCKS WEST MIDLANDS

Much of Birmingham and its surrounding areas was thrown into chaos yesterday afternoon, as an unexpected thunder storm carrying 145mph winds swept through the region.

Locals reported trees being uprooted, trucks toppling and roofs blowing off as nearly three inches of rain fell in just over two hours.

Meteorologists at Birmingham University pinned the blame on a freakish cold front that swept in from Scandinavia, colliding with warm air moving up from the Gulf Stream. Several people were injured and at least one Rack Russell is still missing.

Local shopkeeper Lester Givens said,

'It was dead scary like. At one point, I thought me bloody windows might cave in'.

Word.

Yo yo, did you hear about Ferran? What about him? He turned down Kayla Smart and she smacked him in the face. Shut up. No joke. Knocked him out fully. Where? In the park. Black eye and everything. You serious? Yeah. He wouldn't kiss her, so she smacked him.

That's crazy, why wouldn't he kiss her? I know. Kayla is well fit, you seen her tits? Ennit. I would kiss her all day. I'd do more than that. Get me? What's his problem? Bet he's gay. Must be. What a freak. I know. Wait, I thought Kayla was with Jordan. Nah, they split up. So she's single?

Looks like it. Yo, I might make a move. I heard she gave Jordan a hand job in the Odeon. That's bullshit. Nah, I heard it's true. For real? Yeah. That's so cool.

I know. Ferran could've been in the cinema getting hand jobs and instead he gets beat up and no hand jobs.

I know. What an idiot.

Total freak.

Wake Up Ferran.

I'm outside the Science block, behind the big bins
I can see Lana
she's facing the other way and
I'm desperate to talk to her so I go over and
tap her on the shoulder and she turns around and
she's Kayla and I'm like, what?
Then somebody taps me on the shoulder and I turn round and
it's the back of Lana's head again so I tap her on the shoulder again
and
she turns round and she's Michelle and I don't understand, but
I feel another tap on my shoulder so I turn back and it's Emile
looking at me like what are you doing? So I turn back and
a fist
is flying
at my face.

Bubble.

'Didn't think you'd come'.
Michelle moves books to make space for me, 'Still laying low?'
'Yep'.
'Well you've come to the right place'.
I look around.
The only other people are a few little year sevens for their book club.
I sit down across from her and take out my books. 'Used to come here a lot in year seven'
Michelle smiles. 'Still the safest place in school. Books over people any day'.
And it's the calmest I've felt for a week.
'Where do you want to start? Quadratics?'
She opens the textbook and starts flicking through.
'Why are you helping me, Michelle?'
'Because you need it'.
I stare at her. She stops turning pages.
'Because we're friends'
And I get a flash back of watching her in form room back in the day.

How peaceful she seemed, in her little bubble, reading her book amongst all the noise.

'You alright, Ferran?'

I watch her mouth make the shapes for the sounds.

I watch her nostrils flare a little and her long eyelashes blink.

You are pretty, Michelle, I think. Does anybody ever tell you that?

'Thank you', I say.

She looks away for a second, embarrassed.

'Shut up. You'll make me want to punch you'.

One Knee.

Emile is sitting on the sofa. With a girl.

She is beautiful. Her skin olive and model perfect.

Her dark hair is straight and past her shoulders.

The living room looks shabby around her and, to be honest,
sitting there, holding her hand, Emile looks slightly shabby too.

Her name is Nicole.

She is on her placement year studying Anthropology before
going back to her home town of Marseille in the summer.

And Emile is going with her.

Because they're engaged.

Pastime Paradise.

The cafe door nearly swings off its hinges.

Sophia drops her paper. Dexter and Lenny stop their game.

Mom scans the room.

Stevie Wonder's voice fades out as the song ends.

'Where's your father?' she says, striding to the counter. Patrick is gutting a pumpkin.

'Nina, what a surprise. How've you been?'

Mom slaps the stereo and the music stops. She glares at me.

'You should be revising. Where is he?'

I point at the back door with my knife. She heads that way.

'I think he's actually recording right now', says Patrick.

Mom cuts him in half with a glare and storms through the door.

There's just enough time for all of us to glance at each other,

before she's back out with Dad following her.

'Nina, calm down, please'.

Mom stops dead with her back to him and Dad copies to maintain a safe distance.

'Can we just, take a second'.

Mom blinks slowly, then turns round.

'What is wrong with you?' she says, calm as the Terminator.

Dad looks at me and Patrick, like we can help. 'Nothing's wrong with me'.

She takes a step towards him and Dad actually flinches.

'He's nineteen years old, Theo. He's still a boy'.

She's in that mode where everyone else has disappeared. Dad is still aware we're watching.

'What do you want me to tell you?'

'I want you to tell me that you didn't tell our teenage son that he should drop out of university and throw away his future to marry a girl he has known for less than six months'.

Her tone is like sharpening knives.

'That's not what I said to him'.

Mom takes another step closer.

'No? What did you say then, in all your Theodore Burke sage wisdom? Please, enlighten me'

Dad braces himself for impact.

'I told him to follow his heart'.

The cafe falls into a silence, like that moment before a nuclear explosion when all sound gets sucked away. Then three things happen at roughly the same time;

1. Mom dives for Dad
2. Patrick leaps over the counter to help and
3. Michael calls Mom's name from the open front door

He has Sadie in one arm, fast asleep on his shoulder.

Mom, Dad and Patrick are on the floor. Sophia, Dexter and Lenny are frozen. I'm still behind

the counter with my knife. Everyone is looking at Michael.

'Nina?' he says, stepping in, 'Are you okay?'

Mom picks herself up. Dad and Patrick do the same.

'It's fine. I'm fine'

'What happened?' He holds her shoulder.

Mom brushes hair from her face. 'Nothing. I'm okay'.

She looks like she's going to cry. Dad steps towards her, 'Nina, look'.

Michael steps in between.

'I think we should go', he says.

Dad stares at him and Sadie.

Watching them together feels like when the two star destroyers
collide in Star Wars.

Michael nods at Dad. 'I'm sorry that this is how we're meeting'.

Sadie stirs. Dad just stares.

'Okay then', says Michael. He puts his hand on Mom's back and, as
he leads her out,

she looks at me.

'I'm sorry, love'.

I don't know what to do. She looks back at Dad.

'It's his whole life, Theo'.

Everyone looks at Dad.

Dad just stares.

And it's so typical

that with all the mess I've got going on, and despite the fact

that he's like a hundred miles away,

Emile can somehow still

be the centre

of attention.

YEAR 11.

where you discover what you're made of and
what you're fighting for.

<u>**Playlist.**</u>

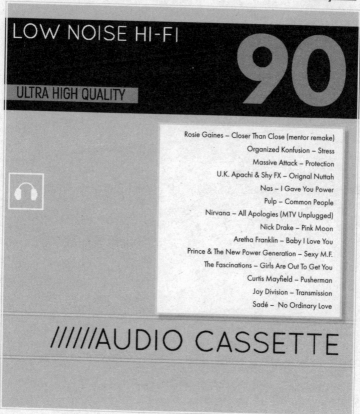

LOW NOISE HI-FI

90

ULTRA HIGH QUALITY

Rosie Gaines – Closer Than Close (mentor remake)
Organized Konfusion – Stress
Massive Attack – Protection
U.K. Apachi & Shy FX – Orignal Nuttah
Nas – I Gave You Power
Pulp – Common People
Nirvana – All Apologies (MTV Unplugged)
Nick Drake – Pink Moon
Aretha Franklin – Baby I Love You
Prince & The New Power Generation – Sexy M.F.
The Fascinations – Girls Are Out To Get You
Curtis Mayfield – Pusherman
Joy Division – Transmission
Sadé – No Ordinary Love

//////AUDIO CASSETTE

Vows. (— means somebody not speaking on purpose)

You're really doing it, aren't you?
I am
—

What can I say, man? I love her
Right
I know it doesn't make sense to you
I didn't say that
Mom thinks I'm mad
No, Mom thinks you're stupid
—

You're not stupid
I dunno. Maybe I am. Maybe I've been hiding it this whole time
I could've told you that
Come here. Damn, you been working out?
Not really. A few press ups
For all them fights?
Shut up.
—

So she must be pretty special
She's incredible
—

I'm just doing what's right for me, you know? For once
For once?
It's my life, Ferran
Trust me, Emile. Nobody's doubting that.

Talent.

She looks tired.

The black cardigan over black dress is a bit funeral and makes her seem older.

On the windowsill behind her, the spider plant is on its last legs.

'Well done', she says, looking at a print out, 'Your end of years went better than expected'.

I picture Michelle, turning round to check on me in the gym before they told us to start writing.

'I got help'.

'Good for you. After your little suspension drama, that's really good to see'.

She closes her eyes as she drinks her coffee.

'Are you okay, Miss?'

'Yes yes, I'm fine. How's Emile?'

'He's getting married'.

Dark liquid sprays across her desk as she spits out her mouthful.

'I'm sorry. What a mess', she starts wiping things down with her sleeve, 'That's, quite a turn of events'. I lean forward and wipe some of the droplets with my elbow.

'Yeah. He's moved to Marseille. That's where she's from'.

'Wow. What about his studies?'

I shrug. She shrugs back.

'Well, what is it they say? Success is a journey, not a destination?'

'I don't know, Miss'.

She rustles some papers around. 'Back to you, Mr Burke. How are you feeling?'

'Okay, I think'.

'A levels?'

Shrug.

'You need to start making some decisions'.

'Yes, Miss'.

'Oh, and I hear you're quite the whizz in the kitchen? Miss Feeney, tells me your food is delicious'.

'It's mostly my partner, Miss. I just stir stuff'.

She wags her finger.

'Don't cover up talent, Ferran. It can light your way better than anything'.

X-ray.

The tension at Mom's is next level.
Her and Dad have been going at it over the phone since Emile left
and it always gets proper *Eastenders*. Whenever I stop at hers, she
talks to me like I'm Dad,
like without him in person I'm the next best thing.
Michael says he thinks Emile and Nicole will come to their senses
before the ceremony, but the fact Emile officially dropped out of
university means Mom
can't even talk about it without losing her shit.
'He's sacrificing his life!'
'He's too bright to be this stupid!'
'He won't make my mistakes!'

I think when something monumentally big happens.
Like a death. Or a divorce. Or your brother ditching his whole life
to move to another country and marry a beautiful girl he just met.
You get
a glimpse of everyone's true self.
It's like the event is so seismic that it rocks the foundations of
the walls people had built up and they start to crack and crumble
down, revealing what's underneath.
Mom being furious.
Dad being quiet.
Emile being Emile.
It's like an x-ray to the bones of them. Who they really are.
And when I turn that x-ray on myself. The film seems to show my
skeleton
is made up of equal parts
of them all.

Level Up.

We're outside the chippy.

Greg is waving his battered sausage around, chasing Amy with it.

Kayla is laughing on Jordan's lap letting him feed her chips.

Lana and Lewis are still inside ordering.

Me and Cello are sharing a bag, watching Taylor do pulls ups on the tree branch.

A group of four sixth form girls walk up. They look like proper women in school fancy dress, all make up and swagger.

Greg stops being stupid.

Jordan stops feeding Kayla and Taylor drops down, fixing his hair.

Just as they head inside the shop, Taylor whistles. The girls look back.

'Afternoon', he says, smiling. Three of them ignore him and go inside, but one of them

with a black puffer jacket and blonde hair, smiles back.

Lana comes out with the chips and sees Taylor.

'What are you doing?'

'Nothing, babe. Just looking'. His grin is pure dismissive.

Lana looks at Kayla, who gets up off Jordan.

'Where you going?' he says, catching the cone as she drops it.

'Pathetic', says Kayla, 'You coming Ames?'

Amy follows them and they walk off back towards school.

'Nice one, Tay', says Jordan, scrunching up his cone.

'Yeah, man', says Greg, 'I was getting somewhere there'.

Taylor just stares in through the shop window. 'Shut up'.

Cello raises his eyebrows and eats another chip.

Selecta.

Chantelle bends over at the stereo and everyone pretends not to notice her thong.

'Which one's the volume?' she says.

'The big circle', says Patrick.

Dad leans in the back doorway, looking slightly anxious.

It's the same light stabby strings, but the dusty drums are speeded up a bit and have more of a swing. Dexter closes his eyes to tune in. Lenny is bopping in his seat.

'You got me up and down, up and down, up and down again'.

Dad's done something to Chantelle's vocals, filtering them a little bit, giving them a slightly metallic feel. It's not exactly Roberta Flack lyrics wise, but it's definitely a groove.

Chantelle sings along like it's karaoke. Patrick nods just about in time.

'Very nice', he says.

'It needs a bridge', says Dad. Chantelle presses stop. 'A bridge?'

'Yeah. Something to break down and build back up'.

Chantelle's eyes widen, 'Like a bass drop?'

Dad smiles, 'If you like'.

Chantelle claps then shuffles over to Dad and hugs him. His embarrassed face is hilarious.

'You're a genius, Theo!'.

She kisses his cheek then checks her watch. 'I've gotta go, can I?'

'Leave it with me', says Dad, 'I'll work on it this weekend'.

'You're a darling. Then we send it to radio stations?'.

'If you want'.

'And you!' she says, pointing at me, 'Lyrical genius!'.

She blows me a kiss and, lost in the moment, I actually reach out my hand and catch it.

Patrick wipes down a table as the door closes behind her.

'So what do you reckon, Theo, future number one?'

Dad smiles at him, 'She's just enjoying herself, Pat. Got a lot on her plate. Working on stuff is like a holiday to her'.

'You're a good man, Theo. Your Dad would be proud'.

They share a moment. I tip flour into a bowl for festivals.

Dexter and Lenny go back to their game.

Stealth.

We're pulling staples out of a tall pile of handouts with the little crocodile pincher things.
Are far as detention tasks go, it's not that bad.
Cage is marking at his desk. Cello keeps pulling faces at him trying to make me laugh.
We write quick lines on the back of scrap paper behind the pile.

I bet he's into bondage
Definitely! Whips and chains
Fully
He has one of them women he goes to
What women?
A thingy. Dominator
Dominatrix?
Yeah! He goes on Wednesday nights She lives in Sparkbrook
What's her name?
Lucy?
No way. Something hardcore
Diane?
Madam Liz
My aunty's name is Liz
Is she a dominatrix?

'Shut up!'

'Something, wrong, Mr Tardelli?'

I feel like the veins in my neck might burst from holding my laugh in.

'No, sir. Just getting it done'.

'Good'.

Take it back!

Madam Liz give gooood spanky spanky. Oooooh

Silent laughing is a fine art. And we're a pair of Picassos.

Fond (– means somebody not speaking on purpose)

So what now, boss?
Nothing. Just keep an eye on it, stir it every now and then, and don't call me boss
Sorry, boss Michelle.
Just watch the pot, stupid. It's all about concentrating on flavour
–

Why are you staring at it?
I'm concentrating on flavour
Stop taking the piss. There's an art in this, Ferran
Yes, Master Yoda
Give it a stir. How's it look?
It looks the same
Does it?
Yeah. Maybe a little darker
Exactly, colour, it's happening. Darker means flavour
Ennit though
–

Sorry
You can add the tomato paste now. Good. Now stir it, coat the veg
Like this?
Yeah. Now once we develop some fond we can add the stock
Develop some what?
Just wait
–

–

281

Yo, it's burning

It's not

It's burning, Michelle, look

That's the fond

The Fonze?

Fond. The bits that stick to the pan. It's the proteins and sugars reacting to the heat.

Like science

Like flavour. It's the stuff you don't see that holds the magic.

Right. Just like you, eh?

—

Do we add the stock now?

—

Michelle?

Yeah. Now we add the stock.

Sunday (and you)

This morning Tuna was following me everywhere/ I went on a
hunt for clean pants/ she followed me/ I heaved a load of dirty
washing from the bathroom/ she followed me downstairs and sat
watching/ as I stuffed the machine and stabbed the buttons/ I took
out the bins
she followed me/ I watered Emile's cactus/ she followed me/ I
made myself scrambled eggs on toast/ she followed/ when I went
to pee/ she followed me upstairs and waited
outside the door/ I couldn't work out what she wanted/ I put food
in her bowl/ I gave her
a stroke/ I opened the back door and pointed outside/ she just
stared up
with her tilted head and
wherever I went she
scampered after/
When I finally sat down
to do my homework/ she sat down
next to my feet and as I took out my folders/ she curled up
on my toes and went to sleep
and I realised/ all she wanted was to be
with me.

Déjà vu.

I'm late again, just less bothered these days.
As I walk past the cloakroom, Lana is crying.
There's no sign of Kayla.
She looks up and wipes her nose. The mascara she shouldn't be wearing is running.
'Sorry. I'll go'.
'No. Stay'.

I sit across from her.
When you're out of class during lesson time, the corridors feel like a different place.
'Aren't you going to ask me why I'm crying?'
'I dunno, when I'm crying, the last thing I want is people asking me questions'.
She wipes her nose again. 'You're kinda weird aren't you?'
I feel myself deflate.
'I mean. You're not like the others'.
'I dunno. Sometimes I feel like I'm a completely different person depending on who I'm with'.

I wasn't expecting to say that. Lana picks at her tissue.

'I know what you mean'.

And the look we share is a new one. A clear one. Real and present.

'He dumped me', she says, popping the moment, 'For that sixth form girl'.

She twists tissue, licks it and dabs the corner of her eye. 'She'll give him what he wants'.

I don't say anything. Last time we sat here I accidentally called her a dog.

'Why didn't you kiss Kayla, Ferran?'.

A flicker book of images plays. Words rush towards my tongue. And I stop them all.

'Because I didn't want to'.

Her surprise turns into a smile and we just sit quietly, on our little cloak room island as

far away

the rest of school

carries on.

What were the six key principles of Woodrow Wilson's 14 Points?

1. Setting up a League of Nations
2. Disarmament
3. Europeans right to rule themselves...
4. History should only be studied by people called Ian or Gertrude
5. Tell Cage's great great granddad to kiss my arse
6. Bun History

Study Hall.

'I can't do it!'.

Cello kicks his textbook off his bed. I'm on the floor with my notes and the past papers.

Mock exams start in a couple of weeks.

'Come on, man. You just need to concentrate'.

'It's bollocks. The P.E. stuff I can get into, even the science bits, but this, this is just dates and flippin, old stuff'.

His room is about the same size as mine, but you can't see an inch of wallpaper

for all the cars and motorbikes.

'Cell, we just need to do enough to get an okay grade. Enough for sixth form. It's like a game. GCSE's are level one. We clock them and sixth form is level two'.

'I'm not going sixth form'.

'What?'

He lies back, staring up at a purple sports car that looks like a Ribena Batmobile.

'Why would I do two more years of school, when I can just get a job and start earning?'

'Doing what?'

'I dunno. Mechanic or something. I could do a course'.

'You still need to pass your exams to do a course'.

He rolls over to face me.

'No. My cousin Marco dropped out in year ten and he works at the KwikFit place'.

'The Kwikfit place? That's what you wanna do?'

'What's wrong with that?'

There's a heavy knock on his door, and without waiting for a
response, his Dad stomps in.

'What's all this, a fairy convention?'

He laughs and strokes his belly and I know it's obvious, but he
really does look like Super Mario.

'Hi, Tony', I say.

Tony scratches his chin and nods.

'We're working, Dad', says Cello, sitting up.

'You should be outside. Not sat in here like a couple of pooftas'.

'Dad!'

'You got a girlfriend, Ferran?'

'Not exactly'

'Right, and I know this one doesn't. So why aren't the pair of you
out there chasing one down?'

I can feel Cello's embarrassment radiating off him.

'We were just saying that', I say, packing up my stuff, 'Weren't we
Cell? Come on'.

Cello follows my lead.

Tony picks at his teeth with his thumb nail.

'When I was your age, I had at least two ladies on the go. They
used to call me Don Juan'.

'I bet they called you some other suff', says Cello under his breath.

'What's that?'

'I said, you haven't lost it Dad'.

'You're damn right I haven't', he pats his paunch, 'Just ask your
mother'.

Cello shudders, as we make our
escape.

Sisters.

'He's not worth it, Babe'
'It's so predictable. Typical man'
'I'll scratch her eyes out if you want me to'
'They all want the same thing'
'You seen her make up? Skank'
'I heard she gave Paul Evans a blow job in The Odeon'
'What a slut'
'Taylor's a Prick'
'He'll be back'

Subtext.

'Time to make your move?' Cello bites his biscuit.

'What?'

He just smiles.

'Shut up. You don't know what you're talking about'.

'Course not'.

We both drink. The hall is full of year sevens and eights.

'It's none of my business' I say.

'None at all'.

'She deserves better than him anyway'.

'You deserve better than her'.

'What does that mean?'

'Nothing'.

A couple of little wide eyed year sevens are watching us from the other end of the table.

I think back to how intimidating year elevens used to seem.

Then I growl at them   and they scatter like birds.

Here Boy.

We have to design a full menu and write about the nutrition of each dish.

Starter, main course, desert.

We'll practise each course then choose our final menu after Christmas.

Miss Feeney went into her speech about food telling a story.

'It's a chance to share yourself', she said.

'What does that even mean, Miss?', said Bryan.

'It means whatever you want it to. Just make your dishes matter'.

'Man', I say, packing up, 'You think she ever eats something that doesn't matter?'

Michelle smiles.

'Toast?'

'Toast matters, Ferran. Good toast anyway'.

'Beans?'

'Same'.

'Weetabix?'

She laughs and my work is done.

'You wanna work on it together?', she says.

'Are you kidding? Does a bear shit in the woods?'

'I don't know, depends if she's in the woods when she needs a shit?'

'Touché. What you thinking?'

'We could go library and brainstorm some ideas?'

'Yeah. Cool'.

Lana walks past with Bryan and Susie. 'You coming chippy, Ferran?'

I look at Michelle. 'I was gonna go library, get some work done'.

Lana pouts, 'I could really do with a chat'. She looks Michelle up and down. 'But if you're busy with your girlfriend'

I take too long to say anything. Michelle grabs her bag. 'I'll see you later'.

And she goes.

The twist of guilt in my stomach.

Lana smiles and heads for the door and like a good lap dog

I follow.

Fold.

'What's going on?'

There's papers and letters and accounting spreadsheets all over the kitchen.

Dad and Patrick are sitting at the table looking like they've been up all night.

'Morning, Ferran', says Patrick cracking his neck.

It's Saturday, but they've closed the cafe so they can have a 'meeting'.

Dad groans and rubs his eyes. 'Man I hate this stuff'. Tuna rubs herself against my shins.

'Shall I make tea?' I say, getting out the cat food.

Dad picks up a letter. 'I could use a real drink'.

'Tea sounds good', says Patrick.

Tuna chows down. I fill the kettle.

Patrick starts neatening papers on the table. 'How's school going?'

'Yeah. You know. It is what it is'.

'I see. A philosopher then'.

I make the teas and watch them roll cigarettes.

'What about cooking classes?'

They both look at me.

'People could come to the cafe and learn how to cook. And they pay. You could run like an evening class or something?'

They look at each other.

'It's a bit late in the day, I'm afraid son'.

Patrick offers a smile. 'It's a good idea though, Ferran. Thank you'.

'So that's it? You're just giving up?'

Dad rubs his eyes, 'I know. It hurts me too, believe me, but we have to face facts'.

'It's bullshit'.

'What your Dad means, Ferran, is, it's a numbers thing. They just don't add up'.

He takes out a lighter.

'What would my Nan say?'

Patrick freezes. Dad taps the end of his cigarette on the table.

'Your Nan would say to remember who you're talking to'.

'Yeah? And what about Pops?'

That gets him. His body slumps back into his chair.

Both of them stare at the papers on the table, like two little boys being scolded.

'There has to be something we can do'.

I feel the lava.

'Enough now, Ferran'.

'No, Dad. We can't give up. The Bluebell matters!'

'You think I don't know that?'

'Theo'

'Its okay, Pat, he's forgetting himself'.

Bubbling.

'I am not. You're the one forgetting yourself'.

'Leave it, Ferran'.

Burning.

'Typical, Dad. Just roll over and take it'

'I said enough!' He smacks the table so hard it tips and papers slide onto the floor, Patrick grabs it in time and steadies it. Dad's glare is primal.

'Easy, boys', says Patrick.

But I'm not done.

'Mom knew you were a quitter'.

The shock on his face. On Patrick's face

as I kiss my teeth

and leave.

Rebound.

We're taking free throws. Mr Evans showed us the proper
technique. Spring from the legs, one hand to steady, one to shoot,
extend the arm and push with the wrist.
I'm alright. Way better than last year.
Cello uses two hands and jumps like a frog. Jordan and them are
taking the piss.
'It's Kermit O'Neal!'
'Baby arms Tardelli'.
At one point, Mr Evans laughs along with them and I can fully see
him years ago in our school kit, just another one of the goons.

In the changing rooms, Jordan and Greg are quizzing Taylor about
his new sixth form girlfriend, Leanne.
'How far have you got?'
'I don't kiss and tell'.
'Come on, Tay. Spill it'
Taylor grins and gestures.
'You fingered her!' says Greg.
Cello looks at me and grimaces.
'What did it feel like?'
'How long do you do it for?'
'Did she like it?'
They're like a radio station I don't want to hear, but can't tune out
of.
'You're so jammy. Amy won't even touch it'.
'Year eleven girls are so lame'.
'You really hurt her', I say.

They all stop. Taylor looks at me. 'What's it to you?'

There's little spots on his broad chest. I rest my towel on my shoulder.

'Nothing. But, maybe you don't have to broadcast private stuff all over'.

He smiles and pulls on his shirt.

'You got a problem, Ferran?'

I can feel Cello's nerves next to me.

'I'm just saying. You were together a while. It just seems kinda lame.'

'Shut up, Burke', says Greg, 'Just cos you're still running away from it', he holds up his hands, 'Don't hit me Kayla, please!'

They all laugh, except for Taylor, who just stares. Then starts doing his tie.

I turn back to Cello and carry on getting dressed as they all dive back in.

'You reckon you'll do it soon?'

'Her parents are away this weekend'.

'Proper?'

'Holy shit!'

'You got johnnies?'

'What about her mates? You need to have a word. Sort us out'.

'Sorry, boys. Only real men. No little boys allowed'.

Eavesdrop.

Dad answers the phone and
right away I know it's Emile.
I sit on the stairs and listen in.

How's things?/I see/What do you mean?/
Okay/Right/Right/That's good/
Why not?/Okay/And you're settled?/Right/Yeah/I think so/And
the planning?/
Right/Yeah/Yeah/Well your mom will want details/I think it's
better you call her/Yeah/No/All good/Hold on I thought I heard/
'Ferran?'
No/No/He's upstairs revising/Yeah/Carry on/
I'm just closing the door.

Classic Dad.
No mention of the cafe closing. Nothing about him and Mom and
their cold war.
Nothing about me.
Classic Emile.
We don't know a date yet, or a location, how to get there, where
we'll stay or whether we're all even invited. Anything.
Emile is basically the tornado the rest of us
clean up after. And Dad is
an empty bench.

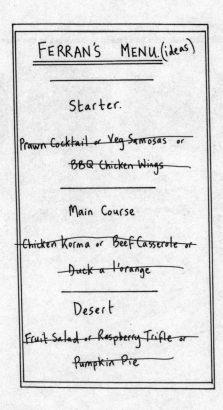

FERRAN'S MENU (ideas)

Starter.

~~Prawn Cocktail or Veg Samosas or~~
~~BBQ Chicken Wings~~

Main Course

~~Chicken Korma or Beef Casserole or~~
~~Duck a l'orange~~

Desert

~~Fruit Salad or Raspberry Trifle or~~
~~Pumpkin Pie~~

Every idea feels lame.

I shouldn't have ditched Michelle like that. But Lana.

I knew she'd want to work alone now. I don't blame her. But Lana.
And I can cook too. I'm not useless.

Who does she think she is? Like she's some kind of cooking
goddess or something and I'm just her stupid human helper? I'll
show her. She's not so special.

Who am I kidding?

She's kitchen Yoda. She's brilliant and her menu will be incredible.
I'm such an idiot.

Question 1 is about food, nutrition and health and relates to the snacks shown below.

A
50g
Chedder Cheese
on
25g white toast

B
50g
Otange Marmalade
on
25g white toast

C
50g
Baked Beans
on
25g white toast

D
50g
Grilled Tomatoes
on
25g white toast

Underlings.

'So we all agree that ambition is a powerful motivation?'

Mr Kelsey is talking about Cassius. I'm sitting on Lana's table.

I'm still struggling with the Shakespeare language, but when we discuss people's reasons, I feel more confident.

'Not as powerful as jealousy', I say.

'Interesting, Ferran. Tell me more'.

I wasn't expecting that. Kayla and Lana look at me.

'I dunno, sir'.

He writes Jealousy and Ambition on the board then turns to us.

'And are they not the same thing?'

People murmur.

'No', says Lana. People looked shocked, she's not usually one for answering questions. 'Ambition is about power, jealousy is wanting what somebody else has'.

Kayla shakes her head, 'That can be power too'.

'Yeah, but ambition is thinking into the future, right? Somewhere you want to get to. Jealousy is right there in front of your face'.

'So is power'.

Mr Kelsey is smiling. This is the most either of them has ever contributed to discussion.

'So it's blurry?' he says.

The girls consider it, then agree. Sir looks at me.

'Would you say so, Ferran?'

And for some reason I think of Cello.

'I guess. But not everyone feels like they deserve power do they, sir? Some people think they're not allowed ambition'.

'I see, well this is where it becomes a more sociological discussion, isn't it? Elements of class and politics'.

The bell goes. People start to pack up.

'Right, great work guys. Concentrate on examples in the text of motivations. Remember to reference the question and know your quotes!'

Full Package.

So it seems like I'm about average
from my covert showers research in P.E.
Greg told everyone his grows to eight inches with a hard on, but
he also said
his cousin met the Stone Roses, so.
I'm as tall as Jordan and Taylor and somewhere in-between muscle
wise.
There's still not much going on the facial hair front though and for
some reason I keep getting spots on my back and shoulders.

> I dug out the book mom got me back in year seven and it
> said it's hormonal.
> Cello is shaving every other day, but he's half a head shorter
> than me.
> I guess nobody has it all.

Ella's Legacy.

There's an older boy in a du-rag
sitting at Sophia's usual table
headphones on
writing in his notebook.
He nods as I pass him. I nod back.
Patrick is rinsing kidney beans.
'Think he's one of your Dad's from the college. He was outside
when I opened up. Asked if he could just sit and write. Said he
can't write at home'.
I pull on my apron. 'Did he eat?'
'Said he wasn't hungry. Not sure he has any cash'.
I watch the boy as I wash my hands, his head nodding to whatever
beat he's writing to, fingers playing the air in between scribbling.
I put a pattie on a plate with a napkin and pour a carrot juice.
The boy lifts his headphones as I put it on his table. 'Oh, no, sorry,
I didn't'
'All good', I say, 'Artist fuel'.

Charizard.

The smoke alarm screams.
I'm frantically wafting my tea towel like a drunken Matador as black smoke billows from my oven.
Bryan starts opening windows. Everyone else has their hands over their ears.
'Everybody relax!', shouts Miss Feeney, dampening a cloth and laying it over my charred chicken wings. I set the stupid oven timer wrong.
'Somebody's mind is on other things'.
'Yes, Miss'.
The beeping hurts my skull. Miss is dragging a chair to stand on.
'Mock exams?'
'Yes, Miss'.
Michelle comes over with the broom. People are coughing. She climbs up onto the sideboard.
Lana and Susie are muttering to each other. Michelle holds the broom by the head and stretches the handle up, deftly pressing the cancel button and the screaming stops.

'Phew! Thank you, Michelle', says Miss.

As Michelle climbs down, everyone applauds.

She hands me the broom with a full poker face.

'My hero', I say, hoping she laughs.

She pauses. Then smiles.

'Okay everyone', says Miss, 'Drama over. Back to it. Ferran, I'm not sure these poor things are salvageable'.

'No, Miss'.

'Do you have a back up wings?'

'No, Miss. Sorry'.

'Don't worry. We've all done it. Nothing teaches like a mistake'.

I look at Michelle.

'Yes, Miss'.

Cramming.

A4 paper. Check

Coloured pens. Check

Bun and cheese for sustenance. Check

Motivational but not distracting Massive Attack soundtrack. Check

Being in Emile's room seemed to make sense. Like maybe some of his uni brain waves

from all his studying in here will filter into mine and boost my memory.

Cello's gone to Laser Zone with Jordan and them. They're not bothered about exams.

I told them Dad needed my help with something so they wouldn't call me boffin.

Dad hasn't done more than grunt at me for days.

I don't know why I want to do well.

I mean, everybody wants to do well, what I'm saying is

I don't know why I want to try.

Am I ambitious?

Jealous?

Both?

I'm not sure what it is. Pretty much every subject feels harder than it used to.

Food Tech is the only one that fully makes sense. The only one I enjoy.

So why am I sitting on my brothers bedroom floor on a Saturday, surrounded by books and notes, trying to revise and do well in the mocks?

I think I just want to know that I can.

0 2 Study **Sources B** and **C** in the Sources Booklet.

How useful are **Sources B** and **C** to an historian studying the causes of the Second World War?

Explain your answer using **Sources B** and **C** and your contextual knowledge.

[12 marks]

_____

_____

_____

_____

_____

_____

_____

_____

_____

You should now check the front of the exam paper to make sure you have the correct paper, and you should read through the instructions on the front, but do not open the question paper until you are told to do so

In English I ran out of time.

I felt like I was just getting my ideas together when they said stop writing.

In Maths it was the total opposite. I did what I could and then spent ages doubting myself and scribbling out my working. With the rest, I don't even know.

Not feeling too hopeful, despite my cramming.

It's okay. At least they're over.

I'm just not Emile.

R and R.

In assembly this morning they announced
that Ms Martin is taking something called a sabbatical.
It's not a religious thing, it basically means a long break from work
to figure stuff out.
'I heard she had a nervous breakdown'.
'I heard her husband left her for an air hostess'.
'I heard she got caught with voodoo dolls'.
'I heard . . .'
'I heard'
Is it irony that the place you come to learn stuff is so full of idiots?
Thanks to Alanis Morissette, I'm not completely sure of the
definition.
Maybe it's more tragedy. Hundreds of fools pretending to learn,
growing into bigger fools.
Sounds pretty tragic to me.
As far as I'm concerned, Ms Martin is the smartest person going.
A sabbatical sounds like heaven.

BUN. (- means somebody not speaking on purpose)

What d'you reckon?
It's delicious. Did you make it?
Nah, there's a place near us, it has all the Jamaican food
You should make some yourself
I don't think so. You should though, with your skills
–

–

Why did you choose Food Tech, Ferran?
What do you mean?
I mean why take it as an option?
I like food
That's it?
What? Why did you choose it, apart from the fact that you're the
kitchen Don?
I like food too.
Alright then
–

I dunno. Something happens when you're cooking, doesn't it?
It's like, a bubble or something, like, food doesn't care about the
future, or the past, it's just cares about making you happy, right
now, in the moment, like, when I'm cooking, everything else kinda
goes away. You know?
–

Too much?

–

Michelle?

B-Boy.

Bouncing down our road.

I held it down in front of the others, but I am buzzing.

It paid off.

A in P.E. C in French. Double B in Science. B+ in Food Tech.

Bs in English and History and even in Maths! (thanks to Michelle).

Not worth my photograph in the newspaper and it's only the mocks, but it's way better

than I expected and good enough for sixth form.

I can stay on at the school, or I could apply to somewhere else.

Mom's gonna be shocked. I'm going to hers tomorrow and I know she's not expecting much.

She's supposed to be going to see Emile in France over Christmas, so it'll just be me and Dad.

I'm not letting him cremate the turkey again, so dinner is on me.

I'm gonna do the little sausages wrapped in bacon and everything.

Then it's just daytime movies and *Columbo* until Kayla's party for New Years.

I've earned it.

Cage's face when he handed out the papers.

I felt for Cello, but he didn't revise.

Them lot are all going to the park later, but I don't feel like standing around in the cold talking shit. I feel like blasting one of Emile's old jungle tapes, skanking round the house and phoning a pizza. That's my plan.

Private jungle pizza rave for me and Tuna.

Keys out.

I did that.

Michelle helped, but I put in the work and it showed. I can do it. I've got skills too. **B**s! Call me B-Boy.

Open door.

'Dad?'

Through to kitchen.

'Dad. Guess what I got?'

They're at the table with cups of tea like it's completely normal.

'Look who's back'.

Same Old Song.

He doesn't even seem that bothered.

Apparently he was just lying there one night, unable to sleep, so he woke Nicole up and they had a long conversation and realised they were making a mistake. Emile packed his stuff, they kissed goodbye and he left. Just like that.

His hair is shaved short now and he has a little goatee to go with the tash.

'I honestly thought about staying there. By myself. Get a job on the docks. It's a really beautiful town'.

'So I hear', said Dad.

You should have. Is not what I say. What I say is.

'So what are you going to do now?'

'I really don't know. I wanted to come home to sort my head out, you know?'

'Good idea', said Dad, 'Take your time'.

I don't want to find him so annoying, but just listening to him speak and pull

dramatic pained expressions like he's been through some emotional meat grinder .

that nobody else can understand makes me want to slap him in the face.

> He gets up to take his jacket off and I'm as tall him.
>
> He's not even bigger than me anymore.

314

'What about you, little brother?' He says, dropping his jacket over the chair and sitting

back down. Now he's finished offloading, I get my tiny bit of attention.

'Any big news?'

I look at Dad. 'Not that I can think of'

'Okay then, click the kettle on will ya?'

In what year did Jamaica receive its independence from England?

A: 1956

B: 1958

C: 1962

D: 1964

True or False – The United States was a member of the League of Nations?

Which civilisation of the Americas is the source of the belief that the world will end or drastically change in 2012?

A: The Incas

B: The Mayans

C: The Navajo

D: The Haitians

Pink Wedge.

Fuck Trivial Pursuit.
In fact, fuck all board games that aren't Snakes & Ladders.
They're like forced game shows, where nobody wins anything
except an argument.
Nothing brings the dick head out in family members quicker than
a few rounds of Articulate!
Michael's turkey was pretty banging though. Gravy too. I went
back for thirds in the kitchen just to steer clear of Emile's two hour
lecture on the perils of having a romantic disposition.
Mom hasn't stop beaming. I watched her resist bringing up his
studies or his future yet, biting her tongue for the sake of the
occasion.
Sadie got a toy workshop with tools and bench and a little
carpenter's outfit.
Mom's fully anti Barbie.
They got me £100 in an envelope which is pretty awesome, but I'd
gladly hand it back if it meant
I didn't have to stay here another night.

Rackhams. (– means somebody not speaking on purpose)

What do you think?
I think ninety quid is insane
It's supposed to be two hundred without the sale
Who pays two hundred quid for a denim jacket?
It's Ralph Lauren
You don't even know who that is
I think it looks good. Do I look bigger?
You look like a cowboy
Cello
It's great. I'm sure she'll be very impressed
Shut up man. I'm not trying to impress anyone
Course not
I'm getting it
It's your money. Can we go back down to the orange perfume
ladies?
Maybe it's stupid. I could just get the 180s
Yeah, do that
I'm not sure. What are you gonna wear?
I dunno. Whatever's clean?
You never know. Amy might kiss you again
I'm good thanks. She's not my type
What, cos you can be so picky?
I might not even come
You have to. I need you there, I can't go alone
Whatever. I'm hungry. Are you buying the stupid jacket or not?

NYE pt 1. 'The Heist'.

If he hadn't started burning his stupid incense again, it wouldn't have even crossed my mind.

I get dressed early and wait until he's in the bath.

His bedroom door is open so he can hear the new Nas album while he gets ready.

He's going drinking with Dad and Patrick in the Bear Tavern. I'm stopping at Cello's.

His window is open and his stuff is strewn everywhere. I go straight for the video shelf and take down *Rocky IV*.

It's not the same. It's pale green leafy buds in a little clear baggy.

I figure if I take a bit, he'll know, but if I take it all, he might just think he's put it somewhere and lost it. Nas is rapping from the perspective of a gun.

'When I'm empty, I'm quiet, finding myself fiending to be fired'.

I put the video case back and look around. My revision pens and paper are still on the floor in the corner. Just when I was getting used to the space.

'Nice jacket'.

Dad is on the sofa stroking Tuna in his lap. Kick drums thump through the ceiling. The tobacco and papers I stole from his coat pocket are in my bag.

'You look like a bond villain', I say, picking it up.

Dad grins and strokes. 'You like my fish, Mr Bond?'

I hear the bathroom door upstairs.

'Gotta go. See you tomorrow'.

'Happy New Year, son'.

'Yeah. Happy New Year, Dad'.

'You did good. On the exams'

'Thanks'.

'Be careful', he says.

I press my pocket and feel the lump of weed.

'I will'.

NYE pt 2. 'The Prep'

It looks like a white twig.

Cello tore bits off the Rizla packet and rolled little tubes for both.

I didn't even know what a roach was.

'I used to watch Maria do it', he says, running his tongue along the paper'.

We put equal parts tobacco and weed in both. We're sitting on the bench at the edge of the woods and even in the fresh air the smell is pretty strong.

'What will he do when he finds out you nicked it?'

'I dunno. Who cares? He deserves it'.

'So he's properly back now?'

'For now. It's like he just breezes back in and takes centre stage again. Like I don't even exist'.

'You exist to me'.

'Thanks, man'.

'We should smoke one before we get there'

'Shit. I didn't take his lighter'.

Cello smiles and pulls a dark blue lighter out of his pocket.

'Tony likes a cheeky Silk Cut on a Sunday night. You wanna spark it?'

I hold one to my lips as he flicks the lighter.

'Remember to breathe in as you suck, pull it into your lungs'.

It feels like somebody lit a fire in my throat and punched me in the chest.

I cough so bad I drop the spliff. 'I think I'm gonna die'.

'Just breathe', He picks it up and blows off the dirt.

'It's cos we're new. It'll get better'.

I can't stop coughing. My throat feels scratched. The taste is pretty awful. And then the head rush.

'Woah'.

I stare into the darkness of the trees and feel myself spinning, but not in a pukey way.

More like I'm sitting on a record, floating round at just the right speed.

Cello takes a drag and holds it in, then coughs just as much as I did.

'Holy shit!' he passes it back.

'I know, right?' I take another drag. More coughing. More floating.

We both stare into the trees for what feels like a long time.

'Are we high?'

'I think so, man'.

'Shall we just stay here?'

We look at each other.

'Yo, your pupils are massive!'

'So are yours!' He reaches out for my face and misses.

And we both laugh so hard, we fall off the bench.

NYE pt 3. 'Arrival'

Kayla's house is big like Mom's.

There's a fat manicured bush in the middle of their front lawn.

I start to get really nervous as we walk up her path. I don't recognise the music thumping inside.

'Is this a mistake?'

Cello rubs at his eyes with his knuckles. 'We'll be alright. Just don't leave me. Man, I'm so thirsty'.

'Me too. And I'm starving'.

We giggle up to the door and then compose ourselves.

'Let me look after the weed', he says.

I hand what's left in the little bag to him and brush myself down, 'How do I look?'

'Best cowboy in town'.

I'm about to hit him when Jarvis Cocker opens the door.

'Hey! I know you! You're the kid who beat up Clifford Packer!'

He's swaying slightly.

'No. I'm just-'

'Yes he is!', says Cello, 'Bad Boy Ferran Burke in the house'.

And he pulls me inside.

NYE Pt 4. 'Seeds'

The music is awful.

It's all Oasis and brit pop stuff you can't dance to unless you like bouncing up and down on the spot. Kayla's brother and his sixth form lot are in the living room.

Everyone seems older than us and I'm feeling well awkward as I follow Cello to the kitchen.

It's shaped like Mom's, but bigger with a conservatory bit and a full pool table.

The light hurts my eyes. Cello is squinting too.

'It's Boffin and Baldrick!' says Greg.

He's by the fridge with Jordan and Lewis drinking cans of Stella. They laugh.

I give him the finger and feel myself relaxing a bit, then I spot Lana with Amy over on a sofa.

'Why don't you take a picture, Burke?' says Jordan.

'Shut up. Where'd you get the drinks?'

He points to the fridge. 'There's loads in there'.

Cello takes two cans out and hands me one.

'What about the weed?'

'What weed?' says Greg. Cello gives me the shut your mouth look.

'We smoked it already'.

'You're full of shit. You didn't smoke any weed'.

'Nah. You're right. I'm just bullshitting'. He cracks his can open. I do the same.

Then a hand grabs my shoulder.

'Nice jacket!' Kayla looks twenty one.

She has on full make up and her white vest is skin tight and low cut showing off proper cleavage.

'Thanks', I say, keeping my eyes on her face, 'You look nice'.

She squeezes my arm and smiles, then she goes over to Lana and the others.

'Did you see them?' Greg's mouth is hanging open like a draw bridge.

'Man', says Lewis.

Jordan stares over as he swigs. 'I'm getting them tonight'.

'Tune!' shouts a guy with messy hair as 'Park Life' blares out from the living room and there's a mini stampede.

Cello looks at me. I shrug and sip my beer.

NYE pt 5. 'Reflection'

We're on a little wall next to a pond with a trickling water feature.
It's only half ten.
'That thing's making me need toilet', says Cello.
He's finishing the Pringles we grabbed. I'm watching a guy inside
in a pink shirt, downing a big glass of something purple while a
circle of people cheer him on.
'Is this fun, Cell?'
Cello lifts the tube to his mouth and tips out the last crumbs.
'Dunno. What were you expecting?'
'I don't know'.
'Are you gonna speak to her?'
People inside cheer as the guy finishes and dances holding his
empty glass on his head.
'Probably not'.
I tip the rest of my can out onto the grass. 'Is this our tribe?'
'Our tribe?'
'Yeah. The people we belong with?'
He pushes the lid on the Pringles tube and stares at it.
'I don't know, Ferran. Maybe we don't belong anywhere'.
Light from inside reflects in the pond water. I throw my arm round
him and squeeze.
'Let's bounce'.
'Yeah?'
'Yeah. This isn't us'
Cello smiles. 'Is this us?' He says, holding up the other joint.
Then the back door opens.

NYE pt 6. 'Happening'

She's wearing baggy khaki trousers and shell toes, holding a mug that says I ❤ Dad.

'Is it weed?'

I look at Cello. 'Yeah'.

Cello gets up. 'I need to pee. Stupid fountain. I'll get more drinks too'.

He heads inside. The shitty music muffles again as Lana sits down. I hold out the spliff.

'I'm not sure', she says.

'That's alright. You don't have to'. I take another drag, 'What's in there?'

She looks into her mug. 'They made a punch. It's pretty harsh'. She takes a sip, 'Swap you?'

It's way too sweet and really strong.

'Nice', I say.

Lana takes a drag and starts coughing. I pat her back. 'Sorry. It's pretty bad isn't it?'

She smiles in-between coughs.

'Where did you get it?'

'I stole it from my brother. He's probably gonna kill me'.

I sip more punch and feel it burn my throat.

'Wasn't he like some super brain genius or something?'

'That's him. Emile Burke. Future World Leader'.

She takes another drag and coughs again. 'What does that make you then?'

We swap back. She's looking at me.

'I'm just Ferran'.

'Ferran Burke'.

'Yes, Miss'

'Well, stand up, Ferran Burke'. She gets up and holds out her hand, light dancing in her eyes.

'What?'

'Come on. I want to give you something'.

My stomach's doing flips as I stand.

Lana sways. 'Woo, my head is spinning'

Her eyes are about the level of my nose. I think this is actually happening. No streetlight or rain. In a garden by a pond. My first kiss. With Lana Jacobs. I try to make out the song to remember it, but I can't. 'Is this happening?'

Lana smiles and puts her hands on my shoulders, 'Yep'.

Then she leans in, closes her eyes and

pukes.

NYE pt 7. 'Flash'

I'm scrubbing at the bathroom sink.

I got most of it off my jeans, but the jacket took the worst of it.

Mental note: Any time you want to snap out of any kind of buzz and sober up quickly, get someone to throw up all over you.

Lana just stared at me in disbelief, then ran inside.

Amy took her into the downstairs toilet and the kitchen was busy, so I came up here.

Luckily most people were too drunk to notice.

Lewis was talking to a pot plant by the front door. I couldn't see Cello anywhere.

They've got the soap that you squirt and I've emptied half a bottle, going at it with a nail brush. The smell seems like it's gone, but I think I've blocked the plug.

Stupid fucking weed. She was going to kiss me. She really was. I was so close. This is Emile's fault.

Somebody knocks at the door.

'I'm in here! Gimme a sec!'

The door starts to open. 'Hold on!', I leave my jacket and go to block it, but Kayla comes in before I can.

'Sorry. I just. My jacket. I used some of your soap'.

She smiles and closes the door behind her.

'Did you kiss her?'

'What?'

'She said she was gonna kiss you'

'Who? Lana? She threw up'.

Her eyes are drunk. The tap is still running.

'But you wanted to, didn't you?'

She steps closer.

'Kayla. I'm not. I should probably go'.

'Why her, and not me?' She hiccups.

'Kayla. Listen'

'She hasn't got these'.

She holds her boobs. I don't know where to look. The music downstairs. The tap is still running.

'Kayla'

'Has she?'

Then she pulls down her vest and bra and just stands there, chest out. My heart is pounding.

'What do you think?'

I make noises that aren't words. Kayla steps closer with her boobs.

'You can touch them if you like'.

She's right in front of me now. The sink starts to over flow. I lean back and stop the tap.

'Kayla, we should get a towel. The water. It's wet. Oh my God'

'Go on'.

She reaches out and takes my right hand, 'Don't be nervous'.

Her skin is warm. So warm. And soft. I can feel her nipple against my palm. Kayla smiles.

'Pretty good, right?'

I nod and she makes my hand squeeze gently. I feel like I'm floating.

'Wow'.

She reaches down. 'Oh, hello'.

Her hand starts to move, squeezing and rubbing me through my jeans. Her pupils are like saucers.

'Kayla, wait'.

'I know what you want'.

I pull my hands away from her chest. 'Kayla'.

She stops. 'What? Did I do it wrong?'

'No. I just. I'm sorry. You're drunk. And. Can we stop?'

'God!' She whacks my chest, 'What is wrong with you, Ferran?'
She steps back and fixes her top.

'No. Kayla. It's not. I'm sorry. I'm just. I'm just-'

'You're just a freak!'

And she storms out, slamming the door, leaving me
and my stupid jacket in her bathroom
alone.

NYE pt 8. 'Cheap shot'

I can't find Cello.

Lewis is still talking to the plant. Greg is bouncing up and down with sixth formers in the living room. Amy is still helping Lana in the downstairs toilet. I check the garden.

There's three different couples kissing and the guy in the pink shirt passed out by the pond.

It's nearly midnight.

There's a side door that must lead to the garage. I go through and click on the light.

There's a murmur from the other side of a big black jeep. 'Cello?'

He's on the floor next to a puddle of puke.

'Yo! What happened?'

He slurs something about punch. I help him sit up. 'We need to leave'.

I get him into the kitchen and pour a glass of water. 'You okay to walk?'

'I'm fine. You're so special, Ferran'.

'Stop talking. Drink. We've really gotta go'.

'Fuck did you do, Burke?'

Jordan is right in my face. I'm holding Cello up against the sink, wet jacket under my other arm.

'What? Back off man'.

'What did you do to Kayla?'

'Nothing'.

'So why's she upstairs crying then?'

Cello giggles, his head dropping forward. Jordan points at him, 'Shut the fuck up, grease ball'.

331

'Fuck off, Jordan'. Greg shows up behind him. I feel the lava.

'Move'.

'You're not going anywhere til you tell me what you did to Kayla'.

Cello lifts his head. 'He doesn't like, Kayla, stupid'. He waves his finger in Jordan's face.

'Don't touch me, gaylord'.

People are counting down to midnight in the living room. 'Ten. Nine. Eight.'

'Move now, Jordan'. 'Five. Four'.

I push past him and see Kayla standing in the hall way, streaks of mascara on her cheeks.

'Two. One. Happy New Year!'

Then something hard hits me in the back of the head and I fall.

A small aside.

You hear people talk about the calm after the storm.
Those few minutes after the event, before you click back in to the
noise of the world.
It's like the seconds of space when the needle reaches the end of
the record, before it lifts
and travels back over to its bed.
Not silence, just muted. The space between breaths.
Sitting on the curb, watching blue light flicker on dark trees
as figures hurry around
like a moving photo.

NYE pt 9. 'A & E'

Dad is filling out forms at reception.

Cello is on my left sipping his black machine coffee. Emile is on my right holding my jacket.

I'm in the middle with my head bandaged, six butterfly stitches behind my ear.

Jordan's face when he saw the blood. Him passing Greg the Stella can to hide.

There's an old guy with a beard asleep across chairs in the corner. Bill Joel is on the stereo.

Patrick comes in through the sliding doors.

'Finally found a parking space. How's the walking wounded?' I look at Cello. The coffee is bringing a bit of colour into his cheeks. His shirt is flecked with my blood.

'I'm okay'.

Patrick winks at him, 'Good thinking to phone the pub'.

Dad comes over. Cello sits up. 'I'm really sorry, Mr Burke'.

'It's okay', says Dad, 'I spoke to your mom.. You're fine to stop at ours'.

He looks at me, 'You alright?'

I nod.

'I hope she was worth it', says Emile, slipping my jacket on, 'Yo, this is really nice!'

I don't tell him about the puke. Dad's already at the door.

Patrick puts his arm round me and we all shuffle out.

NYE pt 9. 'Epilogue'.

By the time we get home it's half three.

I sit with Cello on the sofa. My head is throbbing at the back.

Emile goes to put the kettle on. Patrick goes to use the loo. Tuna
comes in and stares at Cello.

'You're in her spot', says Dad clicking on the fire.

Cello shuffles over and Tuna jumps up in between us. I stroke her
chin. Dad drops into
the armchair and takes out his cigarettes.

'You want to talk about it?'

The lamp glows like lava.

'No thanks'.

Emile brings teas and his guitar and sits on the floor, strumming.

'Is that "All Apologies"?' says Cello. Emile smiles. 'Good ears'.

'Happy New Year to you too!', says Patrick, coming in and sitting
by the fire.

We all sit quietly with our teas.

I close my eyes and see Lana, standing in front of me, leaning in.
Then Kayla pulling down her vest.
Then Jordan and Greg and Mom and Sadie and Michelle, hands in
a bowl of flour smiling.
'Play something, Pat', says Dad, snapping me out of it.
'Oh, I don't know, Theo. It's been a while'.
Emile hands him the guitar and Patrick takes it with the same care
you'd show a baby.
He starts plucking and strumming at the same time. Emile is
watching his fingers. Dad smiles.
When Patrick starts singing, me and Cello look at each other.
'So it written and a so it say, Pink Moon is on its way'.
His voice is amazing. Low and soft, but kind of husky.
My head still hurts, but the room feels warm and safe
and I feel like laughing and
crying at the same time.

Spring Rules.

I don't speak to Jordan and them. They don't speak to me.
Cello speaks to them, but only if I'm not around. I sit by myself in
English.
Lana hardly speaks to me. Her and Amy aren't talking to Kayla.
Kayla won't even look at me. Her and Susie sit by themselves at
lunch.
No more chippy.
At break times me and Cello either swerve the hall all together, or
sit with the year sevens.
All the talk is about A Levels and BTEC and GNVQs and National
Records of Achievement.
Emile always said school was a game, but these days
it feels more like a job
I didn't even apply for.

Greco-Roman.

I come out of the showers and my towel is gone.

Everyone else is getting dressed.

I cover myself up with my hands when Mr Evans walks in. 'Which bright spark lost this?'

He's holding my towel. It's wringing wet.

Cello's face tells me who did it.

'It's mine, sir'.

'Well do you want to tell me how it came to fall out of the window?'

I look over. Greg and Taylor are sniggering.

'No sir. Sorry. I must've put it on the thing'.

'I think I've got an old spare in the stock cupboard. Hold on'.

He walks out.

'Looking a bit cold, Burke', says Taylor. He's naked from the waist up.

Him and Lana are a couple again. Don't ask me how. I walk to my bench.

'Your mom's a bit cold'.

'What d'you say?'

'She's not returning my calls'

He's over in a flash. I turn round and we square up, me still covering myself.

'Nobody talks about my mom', he says, puffing up.

'Fine', I say, 'Will you just tell her to come pick up her knickers then?'

I hear gasps. Taylor grabs my throat. I grab his wrists. He's half naked. I'm fully skin.

Cello is watching.

'What's this?' Mr Evans is standing there. Taylor lets go. I take the old grey towel. It smells like school. 'Nothing sir'.

'No, sir. Nothing'.

Everyone carries on getting dressed.

'I would've stopped him', says Cello quietly, buttoning his shirt as I pull on my pants.

I glance over at Taylor.

'Yeah. Right'.

Minion.

'Have you even moved?'

'Sshhh. I'm winning'.

I drop my bag and sit down. Tuna is curled up in her spot next to him.

The time runs out and the bong sounds. Both contestants have seven letter words.

'Eight', says Emile.

The woman with the dictionary is looking something up.

'Achieved', he rubs his hands together, 'That's fifty nine points to me. I could go on, be a champion'.

'I think you should'.

'Shut up'. He holds up his empty mug, 'Two sugars, please'.

I don't move. 'What time's Dad back?'

'Dunno. They've got a meeting with the bank'.

He waves his mug. Carol Vorderman chooses numbers.

'I can't believe it's gonna close', I say.

'What, The Bluebell?'

'Yeah'

'I know, but what you gonna do? People want fast food these days.
You putting the kettle on?'

'What do you care about, Emile? Besides yourself?'

'Oh, chill out, Ferran. Life goes on'.

Lava.

'And is this your life now, sitting at home watching gameshows all
day?'

'Maybe it is. What do you care? Oh, Mom needs you to babysit
Saturday'.

'What? Why can't you do it?'

'Not really my thing, plus I'm going out'.

Bubbling.

'Maybe I'm going out'.

'Right. Off to smoke my weed, yeah? I told her you'd be there for
six'.

'Prick'

He looks shocked for a second,
then smiles.

Personal Qualities.

I am quite a confident and independent person which allows me to focus, complete tasks and work well in different situations. I have a keen interest in most subjects and a drive to learn new things. I work well under pressure and have always been able to think on my feet to evaluate and thrive in new environments.

I am also a pretty top notch bullshitter, capable of saying just what teachers and other adults want to hear to get them to ignore me and stop pretending they care.

Where do I see myself in five years time?

Hopefully a long way from anywhere that needs me to fill out stupid forms or listen to pointless lectures on my future from bitter people who wish they weren't so old and shit.

Stomper. (– means somebody not speaking on purpose).

Maybe I'll do stuffed peppers
Okay
They could be nice, some feta cheese, few spices
Yeah
You think it's boring don't you?
—
I know. Lame. Why I can't I think of anything?
I think you're over thinking
I need music. I work better with music. If I could blast some Aretha
Franklin or some Prince
Why don't you ask if you can bring a stereo?
Funny. Do you even like music?
Of course I like music. Who doesn't like music?
I mean good music
And what's that? Prince?
That's a start. What you into?
My mom used to blast Motown when she cooked
Your mom?
And old Northern Soul stuff. That's where she met my dad,
dancing
Wow.
There was this one song, by the The Fascinations. Do you know
them?
No. What was it called?
'Girls Are Out To Get You'. On a Sunday morning she'd play it so
loud it filled the whole house and I'd wake up and smell cobbler
Cobbler?

343

It's like crumble, only better. She used to use pink lady apples.
They're these super sweet apples that melt when you bake them. So good

That sounds pretty special

It was

So is it just you and your dad now?

Yeah

And do you still blast music when you cook?

No. It makes him sad.

—

—

Will you come somewhere with me, Michelle?

What?

There's a place. It won't be there much longer and I'd like you to see it before it's gone

Where is it?

We'd need to get a bus

Together?

Forget it. Bad idea.

No. I just. Okay

Yeah?

Yeah

Great. Are you free on Saturday?

Old School.

It feels like when they used to put us in pairs for a school trip.
I got on the bus first and I didn't know whether she'd want to go upstairs so I went to the back.
It's just old women with tartan shopping trolleys and us.
Michelle is wearing dungarees and Doc Martins.
I'm wearing my grey hoodie and my battered 95s.
'Are you going to keep the suspense up the whole way?'
I smile out of the window. 'Pretty much'.
A old lady with blue hair sits down across from us and holds her bag in her lap.
She has the oldest hands I've ever seen. Michelle smiles at her. The lady just stares.
'My first husband was black', she says. My stomach drops. Michelle squirms in her seat.
The woman nods to herself. 'Fantastic man. Good with his hands'.
'Okay!', Michelle springs up and starts walking down the aisle.
We're still a good few stops away, but I follow.
The woman touches my arm as I pass. 'She looks happy with you', she says.
I manage a smile.
The bus doors hiss as they close. The old woman waves through the back window as it pulls away.
I wave back without thinking. Michelle looks at me.
And we laugh.

Hub.

Curtis Mayfield is singing.

Sophia is doing the crossword in the paper. Dexter is shuffling dominoes on the table.

Patrick is handing Lenny teas over the counter. They all look up when we walk in.

'Brother, Ferran!'

I can smell something sweet.

'Who's your friend?' says Patrick.

'Everyone, this is Michelle'.

Everybody waves.

Michelle waves back and I watch her eyes darting around like we're in Aladdin's cave.

'Come in. Come in', says Patrick, 'You hungry?'

The smile on Michelle's face. 'What is this place?' she says.

The pride in my chest. 'This, is The Bluebell'.

We eat pumpkin pie and drink tea. Michelle asks Patrick a hundred questions about the spices and different vegetables. Sophia gives her a brief social history lesson on the cafe. I break down the perils of scotch bonnets. Dexter keeps calling her Lady Michelle.

'These photographs are amazing', she says at one point, 'Who took them?'

Patrick points at me. I get embarrassed. Lenny nods. 'Boy have talent, fi real'.

Michelle looks at me and smiles. 'Sometimes'.

When Dad and Chantelle come out from the studio, Patrick's got us in aprons behind the counter washing and chopping okra.

Michelle's never seen it before and keeps smelling it and stroking the skin.

'Who's this?' says Dad, coming over.

Sophia calls from behind her paper. 'Michelle. The friend'.

'Well hello, Michelle the friend', Dad holds out his hand, 'I'm Theo, the father'.

'Nice to meet you', says Michelle as they shake.

'Tell them, Theo!' says Chantelle, clapping her hands. Dad steps back. 'That's okay, you go ahead'.

'Okay, okay. Everyone, guess what?' She pauses for effect, her red trousers look like

they're made of plastic and her hoop earrings nearly reach her shoulders.

'They played us on the radio!' She squeals and bounces up and down.

'"Local" radio', adds Dad, doing the finger quotations thing.

Michelle looks at me.

'Chantelle is a singer', I say, 'Dad's producing for her'.

'Wow. Congratulations, Chantelle, and nice to meet you'.

'Thank you, Bab. I'm so excited! Your eyelashes are incredible, did you do them yourself?'

Michelle looks away. Chantelle shuffles back out to the studio.

Dad looks at us all.

'It's just PCRL. Remember Justin, from the rap crew? His cousin works over there. He's putting it in rotation for the week, so her family and friends can hear it'.

Patrick nods. 'Brilliant'.

Dad grabs a couple of patties and heads back out. 'Nice to meet you, Michelle'

347

'You too', she says, going back to the okra.

Just before he shuts the door, Dad looks at me and smiles.

We stick around for Saturday soup.

I pour us pineapple punches. Patrick puts Sadé on the stereo and sits with us.

'This is incredible', says Michelle, 'The heat, the sweetness, just wow'.

She looks at me. 'You're so lucky. It's like you have a whole other world in you'.

Patrick grins. I don't know what to say.

'You're pretty good in the kitchen, Michelle', he says, 'If we weren't closing I might've offered you a job'.

'What? No! You're closing?', she looks genuinely distressed, 'Why?'

'Money', says Dexter, 'The route of all evil'.

'But', she's looking at me, like I can do something. 'I know', I say, 'It's rubbish'.

Patrick runs his spoon around the edge of his bowl.

'There are no failures. Just chances to choose'.

It's one of Nans.

Michelle finishes her bowl. 'At least you know your menu for school is sorted now'.

'What?'

She points at her bowl, then all around us. I shake my head.

'Nah. This food isn't for school'.

'Why not? This is you. This is what matters. And this place is closing'.

'That's not the point'.

Her face goes fully stern, 'Ferran Burke. If you don't cook this food

for your coursework, don't ever speak to me again'. She stands up.
'I'm going to the loo, then I need to go home'. Everyone watches
her go upstairs. Then they all turn to me.

Dexter and Lenny holding their dominoes. Sophia peering over her
paper.

'Oh, I like her', says Patrick, smiling.

'I like her a lot'.

Reality Bites.

'What do you want, Ferran?'

A shoal of year sevens splits around us, then reforms.

'Can we talk?'

'About what?'.

'I just. Will you wait a second'.

We reach the cloakroom. 'Lana'.

She stops and turns round. 'What?'

'I wanted to speak to you, about what happened, at Kayla's'.

'That was weeks ago'.

'I know'

'I'm with Taylor now'.

'I know that too. But he's a dick'.

'I'll tell him you called him that'.

'Tell him. Dick'

'You don't know him like I do'.

'I know him enough to know he's a dick'.

She pulls me into the cloakroom.

'Look. I don't know what you want me to say?'

'I want you to tell me the truth'.

'The truth is, I was drunk. It was stupid. I'm sorry I threw up on you'.

'I'm not'.

She sighs. 'Kayla still hates me'.

'She hates me too'.

'You're really not that smart are you?'

'Lana, look, I really think-'

'Ferran. Just stop. Please'.

'But you were going to kiss me! That means something, right?'

She's shaking her head.

'It doesn't mean anything. I'm with Taylor. End of'

'But he dumped you like rubbish, and now you just run right back? How can you be so stupid?'

She looks like she's either gonna burst into tears or slap me.

'Lana, no. I'm sorry. I didn't. You're not. Lana. Wait'.

But she's already gone.

Mercy.

My hands are dripping.

Stupid hand dryer in the toilets never works.

The lunch time corridor rush has already died down.

I'm gonna be at the back of the queue.

As I walk past Cage's room I get myself ready to give my customary middle finger, then I see him through the glass, sitting by himself.

I stop and double back, standing out of view.

He's at his desk, leant over, head in hands.

Probably been reading more of his depressing war poems.

I could burst in and scare him shitless, but there's nobody here to witness

and make it worth the detention.

But if I just smack the door and run off, I'll have the personal satisfaction

of scaring him and also getting away. Perfect.

But I don't.

There's something about the way he's sitting that makes it feel wrong.

He looks different.

Smaller somehow.

He's not even worth it.

'Prick'.

I keep my hand low and give him the middle finger through the wall.

Coursework.

Every sheet has to have a perfect border and title with fancy
lettering.
I took me twenty minutes to do one and now I'm scared to write
on it and mess it up.
Michelle's letters are simpler, so she works much quicker.
'Wish we were cooking', I say, taking another sheet. 'This bit is so
dry'.
'Yeah', she says, 'Especially when you work as slow as you do'.
I wait until she's mid letter, then flick the rubber at her, making her
smudge her page.
'You shit!'
'Yeah. That's what you get'.
I look over her shoulder to the front and Lana's table. She's had her
hair cut.
All the girls want to look like Rachel from *Friends*.
'Are you staying for sixth form?' says Michelle, not looking up.
'I dunno. I've been looking around. You?'

'Same. I was thinking about Food and Catering maybe'.

'Sounds good'

'My Dad wants me to do 'proper' A Levels though. For uni'.

'What about Food?'

She shrugs. I get on with my border.

'I kinda want a fresh start', I say, 'Out of this place, you know?'

'Yeah'.

'I saw the leaflet thing for Halesowen, thought it looked alright. You could do food there'.

She looks up. 'Is that where you're going?'

'I dunno. Part of me wants to just run away, sack it all off'.

'So you don't wanna go uni?'.

I pull my best gangster face.

'The streets is my uni'.

And Michelle laughs so hard she actually snorts.

Just Like That.

Mom's in our kitchen. Sitting at the table.
It feels weird. Like she's an actor from a different sitcom
who's walked onto the wrong set.
Dad's on the back step, smoking.
'Hello, love'.
Her hand bag is hanging on the chair. I fetch a glass.
'Your mom just came over so we could talk', says Dad.
'Good for you'. I pour ginger beer. 'Let me guess, his royal
highness Prince Emile and his all important future?'
Dad gives me disappointed eyes.
'Come sit down', says Mom.
'I've got coursework to do'. I put the bottle back.
'Ferran'
'Don't, Mom, okay? I'm sure you two can sort out Emile's life
without me'. I go to leave.
'I'm sick, sweetheart'.
She's stroking the table edge. I look at Dad. He closes his eyes.
'What do you mean, sick?'
Mom forces a smile.
'Sit down, love. Please'.

Dr. Strange.

It's amazing how quickly you can learn when it matters.
Emile brought books back from the library and we have the leaflets
Mom gave to Dad.
In the space of the half term week, we've become fledgling
Neurosurgeons.

Astrocytoma – A tumour in the supportive tissue of the brain
Tumour – An abnormal mass of cells that grow more than they
should, or don't die when they should. AKA , dickhead cells.
Malignant – aggressive dickhead cells that want to spread round
your body and eat other healthy cells
Benign – contained dickhead cells that are cool just chilling in
their dickhead bubble
Grade II – worse than grade I
Metastasis – the process by which the dickhead cells spread to
other organs
Surgery – What mom needs to hopefully remove the tumour
Radiation Therapy – invisible high energy beams of charged
particles they'll fire at Mom's brain after the surgery to kill the
remaining dickhead cells and hopefully not her healthy ones.

She's known for a while.

Typical Mom, she wanted to manage the situation to avoid complications.

They don't know how long it's been there.

What she always thought were head aches, could've been pressure from it growing.

Michael made Mom go for a scan. One of his old friends dropped down dead at work and they found a tumour he didn't even know he had.

Nobody has said it, but we owe him big time.

If they can get to the tumour and it's contained, she should be okay.

If there are complications, like if the tumour has tendrils or is more embedded

than they thought, things could be bad.

Emile started talking about survival rate statistics, but Dad shut him down.

Her surgery is in two weeks.

Michael has taken her and Sadie up to Wakefield to be with Nana Barbara and Granddad Phillip. Nobody is saying out loud what we're all thinking.

Communion.

Nothing stops.
I've noticed that. No matter what happens. No matter if somebody
dies or leaves or if your mom gets a tumour in her brain.
Everything just carries on.
School. Work. TV shows. Night. Day.
The cat still needs feeding. The washing still needs doing. Bills
need paying.
You still get hungry. You still fall asleep.
Emile said the human mind can only imagine so much bad stuff
before
instinct kicks in to protect us. Autopilots for survival, he called
them.
I don't even know what I feel.
It's like I'm under water.
I can hear things, but not clearly.
I keep thinking about stuff that has nothing to do with Mom and
then feeling guilty.
Like my head should be full of her and nothing else.
Cello wanted to come over, but it didn't feel right having other
people in the house.
It's like we need a fortress to beat it and nobody else is allowed in.

She'll be okay.

She's tough.

She has too much bossing around and sorting our lives out to do.

I know it.

She will. She will.

Please, God.

Tuesday. (– means somebody not speaking on purpose)

So?
So what?
Your dishes, Ferran? Which ones did you choose?
Oh, right. I dunno
We're supposed to give our menus in next week, remember?
–

I realised you can just photocopy your sheets. You don't have to do each one by hand
–

Smart, right? I'm doing mine at lunch if you wanna come. You okay?
How did your mom die?
Wow. That's, pretty blunt
Was she sick?
What's going on?
–

Ferran?
She's got a tumour in her brain. My mom
Oh no. I'm so sorry.
–

Can they fix it?

They don't know.

—

I feel like. Man

I was seven. We were driving to Wales, to see my dad's parents.

—

A lorry hit us.

Oh my god.

I don't remember it properly. My dad and me got pretty banged up.

Mom died in the car.

Michelle

I think that's where it comes from, for me, the cooking thing. All my memories of her involve food.

Garcon.

I remember her having flu.
Curled up in a duvet cocoon on the sofa.
I was the doctor who had to check her temperature and refill her
water.
I'm not sure where Emile and dad were.
At lunchtime I made crumpets. It was the first time I'd ever used the
toaster by myself.
I put them down twice so they'd be extra crispy.
The butter glistening as it melted into the little holes.
I put them on a plate and tore some toilet roll for a napkin.
She was so shocked when I brought them in like a waiter and
laughed
when I called her Monsieur instead of Madamme.
She opened up her duvet and let me climb in and we watched
Columbo together
all afternoon.

Sick Leave.

It's Sunday and I'm making tea.
That's become my role.
I went in on Monday and Tuesday after half term, but Dad let me
take the rest of the week off.
I don't know what he told the school.
His role is keeping the music playing constantly so we don't
have to deal with the silence.
Mom's operation is on Tuesday.
Emile has gone into overdrive applying to go back to uni.
He read some studies about the affect of positive mood against
illness and thinks if Mom's happier she'll be stronger.
It's crazy to say it, but we feel
closer than ever.
'There's no sugar', I say, checking the cupboard.
Dad is reading bank letters about the cafe on the back step. 'I'm
fine without'.
'Me too', says Emile, flicking through a prospectus at the table.
There's a knock at the front door.
Emile looks at me. I lift up soggy tea bags. He goes to get it.
'So will somebody buy it?', I say, handing Dad his mug.
'Apparently they've already had two offers. Thanks'.
'So weird to think of somebody else running it'.
'Oh, it won't be a cafe anymore. They want to turn it into flats'.
We both sigh at the thought, then Emile comes back in holding
something
wrapped in tin foil.
'Who was it?' says Dad.

Emile shrugs. 'Nobody there. This was on the step'.

There's a yellow post it note stuck to the top. 'It's for you'.

I know who it's from the second I open it.

The smell is incredible.

I cut us each a slice and we sit with our teas.

It's the same perfect texture as back in class.

The same hint of cherry.

I feel myself smiling for the first time in a while as I watch them eat.

'Wow', says Dad.

Emile wipes his mouth. 'This is the best cake I've ever tasted. Who made it?'

I look at my slice.

'A friend'.

Waiting Room.

Sadie's on my lap.

I'm reading her *Little Miss Sunshine* for the fifth time. Emile is pacing up and down. Dad's feet and hands won't stop tapping. Michael is sitting still, hands on his thighs.

The window is open so the antiseptic smell isn't so bad. Every time anyone dressed in nurses clothes comes by we all prick up like meerkats.

'Worm', says Sadie pointing.

'That's right. The worm. Good girl'.

Michael looks at his watch. Emile comes and sits down.

'What's taking so long?'

Michael speaks calmly, 'It's brain surgery, Emile'.

Emile nods an apology.

Then a woman in light green scrubs and a head scarf walks towards us and

we all freeze.

FERRAN BURKE PREDICTED GRADES GCSE.

SUBJECT	PREDICTED GRADE
ENGLISH LANGUAGE	B
ENGLISH LITERATURE	B
MATHEMATICS	C
SCIENCE (DOUBLE AWARD)	B B
FRENCH	C
HISTORY	B
DESIGN & TECHNOLOGY (FOOD TECH)	B
PHYSICAL EDUCATION	A

Wish.

We're playing snakes and ladders.
It's Christmas holidays. Emile is in year seven.
He's pretending his Vimto is wine to be like Mom and Dad.
I don't understand why wine is better.
Mom keeps correcting me when I say dice. There's only one, so it's pronounced 'die'.
I don't want anyone to die so I keep saying it wrong on purpose.
Dad hasn't rolled a single six so he's been stuck at the start for ages.
Every time it's his go, he blows on the dice for good luck. 'Gotta get one soon'.
Emile explains the gambler's fallacy. How Dad is wrong for thinking that just because he's rolled lots of times and not got a six, he's due to get one. The probability of rolling a six is exactly the same every time, 1 in 6, regardless of how many rolls have gone before.

'Luck has to change', says Dad, rubbing his hands together.

'It's not luck', says Emile, 'It's maths'.

Dad looks at Mom, 'That's your son'.

'Yes he is', says Mom and her and Emile do a cheers with their glasses.

Dad picks up the dice again. 'You mathematicians suck the fun out of anything', he ruffles my hair. 'Us artists believe in luck, right big man?'

He holds out the dice for me to blow on. I close my eyes like it's birthday candles

and wish

for a six.

Exhale. Pt 1.

We have to go in two at a time.
Michael and Dad went in first.
The surgery went well. They have to wait to see if they got it all
out and how her body reacts, but she's stable and sleeping.
Emile and me watch Sadie stacking multicoloured pots in the little
toy corner.
'She'll be starting nursery soon', I say.
Emile nods, 'Yeah'.
He takes a really deep breath
and starts to cry.

Exhale. pt 2.

'Thank you, Michael'.
Michael is holding Sadie. Sadie is drinking juice.
'You're welcome, Theo'.
The two of them stare at each other.
'I'll tell her you were here'.
He holds out his hand. Dad takes it. Sadie holds up her carton.
'Juice!'
Dad and Michael smile.

Cobbler

Pink lady apples
Brown sugar
Cinnamon
Butter
Plain flour
Dark brown sugar
Baking powder
Salt
Milk
Vanilla Extract

Need an
hour and
half.

Miss
Feeney
in
reception

Surprise.

I go in early.
Miss Feeney said they have all the other stuff in the cupboards,
so my carrier bag is just full of the pink ladies.
We've got Food Tech first thing so if I time it right, it'll be almost
baked when people come in.
It won't be as good as her mom's, but I can't wait to see her face.
There's hardly anyone around.
Just a couple of sixth formers and a few scattered year sevens.
I feel that crackle of excitement.
As I come round by reception I see Cage's car pulling in.
He gets out with his stupid briefcase, then leans back in.
There's somebody else in the car.
I don't know which poor teacher agreed to car pool with the
original prick of the staffroom, but I'm keen to see.

Then Michelle gets out.

Dark Side.

He's her dad.
The grand overlord of all dickheads.
Torturer of Cello, Emile, me and countless others.
King Bitter, the supreme being of anti-cool.
Is her dad.
She uses her mom's surname to keep it from people.
It's a sick joke.
The look on her face when she saw me. Dropping the bag.
The apples rolling across the floor.
I feel dirty. I feel cheated. I feel rotten on the inside.
How?
How does someone so cool come from someone so utterly grim?
It makes no sense.
I hate the world.
Fuck you world.
Through the mantle and the magma and all the other shit,
fuck you right down
to your core.

Visiting Hours.

Dad's fiddling with the stereo as he drives.
I'm staring out of the window. It looks like it's going to rain.
'Is it weird that I'm nervous?' he says, flipping the cassette over.
'Me too', says Emile from the back as we pull up to traffic lights.
We're half way to Mom and Michael's.
I see Michelle's face every time I close my eyes.
'You okay, Ferran? Something happened?'
I shake my head. 'Some things just don't make any sense'
He presses play and the grumbly bass of 'Transmission' by Joy
Division starts.
'Took me a lot longer than fifteen years to figure that one out'.
The lights go green and Ian Curtis's flat voice and
something about the sounds and the dark sky all fits.
Dad doesn't have super powers, but he sure knows how to pick
the right song.

Gut.

She's wearing a head scarf
to cover her stitches.
Propped up on like a hundred pillows, she looks thinner.
The radiation therapy knocks her out.
I'm on the chair next to her bed. Dad and Emile are downstairs
with Michael and Sadie.
'What did they say? Is it working?'
'Looks like it. They just want to be sure it's all gone. I have one
more session'.
'And then what?'
'Then I get back to bossing you all around'. She smiles and takes a
second. 'What about you?'
I look across at our reflection in the wardrobe.
'I'm okay'.
Mom reaches for my hand.
'Revising?'

'Kind of. It's exam leave soon. Emile helping me draw up a timetable thing, like he did'.

'Great. And your Dad says you've applied to A levels at a different sixth form?'

'Yeah. Halesowen. It's a bus ride away, but it looks good'.

She squeezes my hand. 'Fresh start. I get it'.

She raises a fist. I do the same.

'I made you a banana loaf. It's downstairs'.

'Thank you, love. That's a good reason to get up'.

She closes her eyes like she might drift off, then opens them again.

'I'm so proud of you, Ferran'.

'What for?'

She opens her arms and we hug so tight I can feel her heart beat against my chest.

'I don't think your Dad's so wrong after all'.

The tears start as she strokes my head and we cry
and we cry.

Little Big Brother.

Up!
You want to come up?
Up!
Okay, come here. There we go
Up!
We are up, Munchkin
Up!
You want to go higher?
Up!
How's that?
High
That's right. You're the highest munchkin in the world
Down
Okay. That better?
Up!

Okay, and, up. Oh my days, you're so heavy!

Up!

I can't go up any more. There's no more up

Why?

Because my arms. They don't go any further

Why?

I don't know why, sorry

Ferran

That's me

Ferran brother

That's right. I'm your big brother

Meal

Emile?

Yeah

Yeah. Meal is okay too.

Clunk.

Me and Emile are carrying a box of Dad's recording gear to the car.
The studio is stripped bare.
We spent the whole day helping Patrick and Sofia pack things up
and clean the cafe.
Dad's arranged for all the furniture and food equipment to be
picked up next week.
End of an era.
No more Bluebell.
I push the box onto the back seat and close the door.
'Did you know Cage had a daughter?'
'I don't think so. Why?'
'Dunno. It's just weird'.
'Right'. He takes out tobacco and starts to roll up. He doesn't hide
it any more.
'He was actually pretty cool when I first started'.
"Cage?'
'Yeah. He used to do loads of cool stuff in class, play old movies
and get us to dress up. Then he was off for that whole year and
came back completely different'. He sparks his cigarette.
'Pretty messed up though, with his wife and that, car crash, right?
What's wrong?'
My throat feels dry. I close my eyes.
'Ferran, you okay?'

Empty.

She's not in.
I sit at our usual table by myself, recipe books open for show,
pretending to make notes about my menu.
My head feels like a broken plate. I can't fit her and him together,
but I miss her.
I miss my tribe.
'Decided?'
Miss Feeney has her hands on her hips.
I hide my blank page. 'Nearly, Miss'.
'Okay, Mr Mysterious. Play it your way, but I hope you've
been practising. I want your final menu on my desk by Friday,
understand? That goes for everyone!', she turns to address the class,
'Final menus, end of the week'.

I pack up slowly and think of Michelle inspecting the okra
like an archeologist in the Bluebell.
The smile on her face.

'Can we talk?'
Lana is standing by herself. Bag on shoulder.
Miss Feeney comes over. 'Are you two staying on to work?'
Lana nods.
'Great. I'm just going to grab my lunch from the staffroom. Watch
things for me'.
She leaves and it's just the two of us
in the Food Tech room.

Closure. (– means somebody not speaking on purpose)

Ferran, I–
Before you say anything, can I just? I'm sorry, Lana. What I said.
You're not stupid
I might be
No. I don't think you are. I'm just. It's been a weird year.
I like you, Ferran
–
I mean, I think you're special
Lana
I'm leaving
What?
We're moving down to Portsmouth. My Dad got a new job
When?
Soon as exams are done
Right

I just wanted to, because next week is exam leave and I didn't want
to go and you to think, what I said. It did mean something. That
you liked me. I just wanted you to know. I felt it.
—

And you were right about Taylor
I'm sorry
I think I just. I don't even know what I think. Brains are weird
You deserve something special, Lana. That's what I think
—

—

Is it weird if we hug?
I don't think so

Then she's in my arms.
Lana Jacobs. Stuff of daydreams. Pressed against me. Saying
goodbye.
And it's fine.

Alarm.

I go to the cloakroom.

Sitting on the same bench where I sat with her, watching everyone grab

their stuff and head home, feels like the right end to the day. To the year.

I feel exhausted, but good.

Clear.

Like I know what I have to do. Like I know what matters. Who matters.

Then Cello runs in out of breath.

'Yo! There you are. Where've you been?'

'Nowhere. Here'.

He leans on a hook, panting. I pick up my bag. 'I need to talk to you about Cage'.

'Forget Cage. We gotta go. Now!'

'What? Why?'

'Taylor'.

Rumblefish.

If I didn't know better
I'd say he's been crying.
Jordan, Greg and Lewis are with him. The empty corridor behind them.
They have us trapped in.
'Fuck him up, Tay', says Greg.
Taylor stares at me with red eyes.
Cello raises his hands. 'Come on, man. Don't do this'.
Taylor glares at him and he backs up against the hooks.
'What's going on?' I say.
Taylor keeps staring. 'You think you're so smart, don't you?'
'What you talking about?'
'Sniffing around her since year nine'. He steps forward.
Greg points. 'Smack him!'
Him and Lewis grin like good evil side kicks. Jordan is hanging back.
'Is this about, Lana?' His eyes twitch at the sound of her name, 'Cos she's leaving?'
'Cos she dumped him, dickhead!' says Lewis. Taylor turns to him and he shrivels.

385

I look at Cello. He's bricking it.

'Let's leave it, Tay', says Jordan, from the back. He wants no part of this.

I step forward, 'Let's go, Cell'.

Taylor blocks me.

'Oh, grow up, man. So she dumped you. You didn't give a shit about her anyway'.

He steps right up. His nostrils flaring. Cello is shaking next to me.

'So I'm a dickhead?' He says. 'She deserves better than me? Better like you?'

And just like that it's clear this is only going one way

and

I feel calm.

Like this is the only ending to our story that makes sense.

So I stare right at him.

'Better like anyone'.

His shock turns to rage. I brace myself, and then

Cello smacks him.

Special.

Empty toilets.

I'm holding damp toilet paper to Cello's eye.

He got the one sweet surprise punch in and I did my best, but they beat us up good.

My lip is split and my ribs are sore.

Cello's nose popped and his eyebrow is cut.

If it hadn't been for Jordan pulling Taylor off, it could've been worse.

The two of us, hobbling down the empty corridor like soldiers across a battlefield.

The drip of the tap echoes.

Cello winces as I press.

'Sorry'

'It's alright'. He pulls the bloody tissue from his nose.

'What were you thinking, Cell?'

'I dunno. But I've been thinking it for years'.

I straighten his tie. 'Pretty dumb'.

We share a chuckle and wince again. I fetch more toilet paper.

'Why did you do it, Ferran?'

'Do what?' I dab his cheek.

'Stand up to Cage that time, with the essays. You remember?'

'Course I do. You know that was my first ever detention?' I check the cut.

'I dunno. It wasn't right, how he treated you. I think it's stopped bleeding'.

'Thank you'.

'All good'

'No', he moves my hand from his face, 'Thank you'.

He goes to the sink.

'It's all gonna change now'.

'What do you mean?'

'I mean, you'll go to your college, meet new people'.

'So will you'.

'You'll be busy'.

'What are you saying, Cell?'

'Nothing. I just. We're different, Ferran. Me and you'

I go over to him. He looks so sad.

'Hey. We're mates. We don't have to be the same for that'.

He shrugs.

'Shut up, man. You're punch drunk. It's making you dramatic. We're not so different, me and you'.

He messes with the tap. 'I don't have what you have, Ferran, you're smart'.

'Hey. Look at me. Oi. Smart is being yourself, and nobody else', I grab his shoulders, 'You hear me? Fuck what anybody else says. Fuck school. Just do you'.

I can see tears in his eyes.

'You're special, Cello. I know it, trust me. Do you trust me?'

He nods.

'So say it'.

'I trust you, Ferran'.

Then he kisses me.

I pull back and
everything stops
We stare at each other
I touch my lips
He breathes out first
Disbelief turns to fear
on his face
'I'm sorry'. He says, backing away.
'Cello, no-'
'Ferran'.
'Wait'.
'I'm so sorry'.
And he runs.

Shot gun.

I'm eating cola cubes,
walking home the way I used to go with Emile in year seven
a dark metallic blue sports car pulls up along side me
the window goes down and Cello is driving
he's older, like eighteen maybe, with a thin dark moustache and
a gold chain over his black t-shirt.
I can hear Tupac's 'I Ain't Mad At Cha'
He stares at me.
I hold out my cola cubes
'Want one?'
Cello shakes his head.
'Okay then', I say.
'Okay'
He smiles half a smile. 'I'll see ya, Ferran'.
then he revs the engine and
drives away.

Saturday

I wake up to Marvin Gaye and the smell of burnt toast.

Emile looks like a traffic cop, wafting smoke through the open back door.

I lean on the fridge and watch him.

Even the smartest people can look like fools.

'I think the toaster's broken', he says.

'Yeah? It was fine yesterday. Where's Dad?'

'He had a thing with Chantelle. Something about a manager'.

He drops his cremated toast into the bin.

'You remember when we used to make dumplin with Nan and Pops, and she'd let us plait them and make shapes?'

'You made the shapes. I kept it simple'.

'Yeah, okay. Will you make some, please? Your ones I mean'.

I take out the flour and he smiles.

'Hold on', I say, 'I just need make a phone call. You're doing the teas'.

Okay.

Hello?

Hi, is Marcello there please?

Who's calling?

It's Ferran

Oh, hello, love. How are you?

I'm okay thanks, Christine. Is he there?

Yeah. One second, I'll go get him.

—

I'm sorry, Ferran. He's actually gone out

Right

Yeah. I made a mistake.

I see

Do you want me to give him a message?

—

Ferran?

Yes please. Can you just tell him, it's okay.

Masters.

'So, I've got a bit of news'.

I'm carefully making sure I've got a bit of bacon, egg, dumplin and beans

on my fork for the perfect mouthful.

Emile is wiping his empty plate with a finger. Dad waits until we look at him.

He's smiling.

'What's happened?' says Emile.

'You remember the track I made with Chantelle?'.

'Yeah, the Yo-Yo one. What about it?'

Dad takes another bite.

"Well, it got a good response on the radio, just the white label, and somehow, it got to Radio 1'.

Emile looks at me.

'Are you kidding?'

'No. They played it last week and a few times since'.

'On Radio 1?' I say.

Dad nods. Emile stares at him.

'Why didn't you say anything?'

'What's to say?' He carries on eating.

'Spit it out, Dad!'

Dad puts his fork down. 'Sony offered us a deal'.

'A record deal? You and Chantelle?'

'Yeah'. He's grinning like a little kid.

'Oh my god!'

'What did you say?'

He picks up his fork again. 'I told them to kiss my arse'.

He chuckles as he eats.

Emile nearly chokes, 'But, Dad! The money! Was it a lot?'

Dad nods. 'Oh yeah'.

'What? How can you? Are you mad?'

Dad just shakes his head. Emile is holding his head.

'What are you thinking? Look at us, we could use that money!'

'I get it', I say.

'Shut up, Ferran! Dad, we need to discuss this, this isn't something you just throw away. Think! What about Chantelle? It's her record too and you're stopping it coming out'.

'Oh, the record'll come out', he pats Emile's hand, 'Don't worry, Berry Gordy'.

Dad smiles at me. I smile back. I know what he's done.

'What did you call it?' I say.

'Call what?' Emile hates not knowing. 'Call what, Dad?'

'The label', I say.

I'm not sure how many times I've sat through the industry lecture.

Advances. Recoupment. Production rights. Masters.

Dad's experiences going through the music industry wringer.

Emile never really paid attention.

He's set up his own label.

All you need is an address to register the company and the release.

He'll put the record out himself, that way him and Chantelle
will own everything.

If they're already playing it on national radio, the promotion has
taken care of itself

and if Sony are sniffing around, the possible royalties must be big.

Big enough say, to save a sinking cafe.

'Bluebell Records', he says, grinning as he takes another mouthful,
'Man, these dumplin are amazing!'

Alchemy.

I'm pulling from all over the catalogue.

I've got some Motown, some Factory Records, a bit of Reggae, some Ska, sprinkle of East Coast Hip-hop, but the jewel in the crown comes at the start of side two.

I managed to find The Fascinations track she mentioned on one of Dad's northern soul compilations.

Tuna stretches and shifts position.

I take off the headphones and give her a stroke.

'What's all this?'

Emile stands in the doorway in tracksuit bottoms, scratching his nuts.

I slip Joy Division back into its sleeve.

'You making a mixtape?'

'Yep'

'And did you make that bun in the kitchen?'

'Yeah. Don't touch it'.

'Why not? It looks good'.

'It's for someone else. Why you up?'

'Couldn't sleep'

'You okay?'

'Yeah. Mad year, eh?'

'Just a bit'.

Both of us nodding. On a level. He sits down and strokes Tuna.

'Who's it for, then, all this?'

I take out Innervisions and give it a blow.

'A friend'.

Coursework.

'This is late', she says, taking my folder, 'I said Friday'.

'I know, Miss. I'm sorry. I've had a lot on'.

'So I hear. How's your mom?'

'She's okay thanks. Tired, but getting better'.

'That's good to hear'.

She pulls out my menu sheet. I watch her read through.

'Miss?'

'And you feel confident you can make all this?'

'Yes, Miss. It's the food I grew up with. Stuff that means the most to me. Is it okay?'

She puts it down, smiling.

'It's absolutely perfect'.

Itchy Feet.

Walking the corridors feels weird.
We'll come back for exams, but only in the sports hall, so this is pretty much
my last day here.
I remember walking round this place feeling so small. So scared.
Seems like such a long time ago.
'Ferran?'
She's locking her door. Her hair is up in a bun, thin billowy blouse
just a regular white.
On the floor there's a box full of books and her spider plant
sticking out the top.
'Hi, Miss'.
'Look at you. Aren't you on study leave?'
'Yes, Miss. I just came to hand something in'.
'You look well'. She picks up her box.
'Are you leaving for good?'

She nods. 'Just collecting my things. Got the travelling bug again'.

'Let me, Miss'.

I take the box and we walk towards reception.

Little year sevens scuttle past into the break time hall.

'Where will you go?' I say.

'Peru. To start. Then I guess we'll see'.

We go out to her car and she opens the boot.

'And you're off to be a farmer'.

We both laugh. I put the box in and she closes it, then pulls me in for a hug.

A bunch of year nine girls stare confused as they head inside.

'Find your tribe, Miss'.

'Thank you, Ferran. I intend to'.

Status Quo.

He's with Jordan and Lewis,
coming out of the changing rooms.
A few people had to come in to finish their physical assessments
for P.E.
I'm sitting on the bench with my tea and biscuit for old times.
Lewis says something. Jordan whacks him and they laugh. Cello is
a step behind.
His face is still bruised.
They all stop when they see me.
Jordan offers a nod. Lewis follows his lead. I nod back. Cello won't
look at me.
'In a bit, Burke', says Jordan.
'Yeah', I say, 'Later'.
When they're a few metres past me, Cello looks back.
My mouth opens.
He shakes his head. Half a smile, then he turns and
follows them inside.

New Page. (– means somebody not speaking because he doesn't know what to say)

Mr Burke

–

I didn't expect to see you

Yeah, well

How's the revision going?

We don't have to do any of the small talk, sir. I need your help

And it's to do with Michelle

Yeah. I need you to give her these. Do you have a cassette deck?

I believe so. And what about this?

It's something I made for her. It's bun. It's best with a bit of butter and sliced cheddar.

Okay

And I need you to tell her that there's a party at The Bluebell on Saturday, all day, and I could really use her help

Bluebell?

She'll know what I mean. I'll be there from early.

I see. Is that all?

I'm sorry for your loss, sir. Your wife. I can't imagine that.

–

Your daughter's special. If she wants to study food, you should let her. It matters

–

I really won't miss this room
—

You made a lot of people feel stupid and scared in here, Sir
But not you though, Mr Burke. Or your brother.
No
And why is that do you think?
That's easy, Sir. Me and my brother, we're not a lot of people.

Just So You Know.

Chantelle and Dad are in the kitchen, talking label plans.

Emile is upstairs with Gemma.

They're not saying boyfriend or girlfriend, but now he's applied to uni here

it might be something.

She seems lovely. Takes the piss out of him and everything.

Her face when she saw the cactus.

'Emile, you kept it? All this time!'

Him flashing me a thank you nod. 'Yeah. Course. It's a metaphor'.

I'm on the living room floor with my big revision sheets.

Emile showed me how to make them.

You use different colours for different areas and spread out the facts, then put them up on your wall.

That way, you see them all the time and so in the exam, you can try and visualise

your wall like a memory, rather than having to conjure loads of faceless dates and details.

He read a study.

I scratch Tuna behind the ears. 'If it worked for him, right?'

There's a knock at the door.

It's Kayla.

She's wearing a black Adidas tracksuit top and jeans. Her hair is in a pony tail.

'Hi', she says.

'Hi. How did you?'

'I followed you. Ages ago'.

'Right'.

I look past her up the road.

'It's just me', she says, 'I'm by myself'.

'Okay. You wanna come in?'

She shakes her head.

'I'm pretty good too, Ferran'.

'Kayla, listen, I'—

Before I can say more she steps up, grabs my face and kisses me. Proper.

Her lips are full and soft and, as her fingers slide back around my head, I feel myself

relax into it   and it

                    is

                    amazing.

When she steps back down, it takes me a second to stop moving
my lips and open my eyes.

'Wow. Kayla'.

She nods. 'See? Your loss'.

She grins and starts backing away towards the gate.

'Kayla, wait'.

'See you around, Ferran Burke'

and she's off down the road.

When I finally turn back inside, Emile and Dad are standing by the
sofa.

'Who was that?' says Dad.

I touch my lips. 'That was, Kayla. From school'.

Dad chuckles. 'Okay, then'.

Emile frowns, 'Nobody ever showed up at our door just to kiss me'.

Dad pats him on the shoulder and winks,

'Guess some people are just special, eh Ferran?'

Ferran Burke GCSE Food Technology.

FINAL MENU

Starter:

Saltfish Fritters

———— * ————

Main Course:

Brown Stewed Chicken with
Rice n Peas, Plantain &
Slaw

———— * ————

Dessert:

Nan's
Rum & Ginger Cake

Epilogue.

'No fuss them too much', says Nan.
Emile is already making complicated shapes with his,
plaiting and twisting strings.
I cut small pieces and roll simple balls. Nan winks at me and smiles.
Pops presses the sizzling plantain into the pan with the back of a
fork. The sweet smell floats
on Miles Davis' trumpet from the living room.
'Double portion of ackee, right Ferran?' He grins back at me. He
knows I hate it.
'We have beans, Ella?'
Nan points, 'English cupboard'.
Pops flips the plantain and fetches a tin of Heinz.
Nan scrambles the eggs. Emile carries over the board with our
dumplin.
His look like jewellery. Mine look like stones.
Pops puts the plantain in the oven to keep warm and adds more oil
to the pan.
The dumplin crackle muffles as he covers them with the lid.
Emile and Nan set the table. Pops lifts me up to stir the beans.
When the food is ready, we all sit round the table as Pops dishes up.

'Big meal for the big boys', he says.

My stomach smiles as I eat.

The plantain is sweet and sticky, the scrambled eggs done just
enough,

orange juice cold and sharp.

Emile shovels up his beans, already thinking about something else.

His fancy plaited dumplin are like fossils, pretty, but hard to chew.

Mine are simple, but fluffy

like crispy coated

clouds.

'The people who give you their food
give you their heart'
– *Cesar Chavez*